the method

Also by Juli Zeh

Eagles and Angels
Dark Matter

Juli Zeh

the method

Translated from the German
by Sally-Ann Spencer

Harvill *Secker*
LONDON

Published by Harvill Secker 2012

10 9 8 7 6 5 4 3 2 1

First published with the title *Corpus Delicti* in 2009
by Schöffling & Co. Verlagsbuchhandlung GmBH, Frankfurt am Main

First published in Great Britain in 2012 by
HARVILL SECKER
Random House
20 Vauxhall Bridge Road
London SW1V 2SA

www.randomhouse.co.uk

Addresses for companies within The Random House Group Limited can be found at:
www.randomhouse.co.uk/offices.htm

The Random House Group Limited Reg. No. 954009

A CIP catalogue record for this book is available from the British Library

ISBN 9781846554278

The translation of this work was supported by a grant from the Goethe-Institut, which is funded
by the German Ministry of Foreign Affairs.

The Random House Group Limited supports The Forest Stewardship Council (FSC®), the
leading international forest certification organisation. Our books carrying the FSC label are printed
on FSC® certified paper. FSC is the only forest certification scheme endorsed by the leading
environmental organisations, including Greenpeace. Our paper procurement policy can be found at
www.randomhouse.co.uk/environment

Typeset by Palimpsest Book Production Limited, Falkirk, Stirlingshire
Printed and bound in Great Britain by CPI Group (UK) Ltd, Croydon, CR0 4YY

For Ben

Contents

The Foreword

Health is a state of complete physical, mental and social well-being, not merely the absence of infirmity or disease.

Health is the unrestricted flow of life in the physical body, through every organ and cell. Health is body and mind in harmony, biological energy achieving its fullest potential without obstacle or interruption. A healthy organism will interact positively with its environment. A healthy human will feel invigorated and capable. He or she will feel invulnerable to infirmity, be mentally vigorous and emotionally balanced.

Health is not static; it is the dynamic relationship between body and brain. Health must be maintained and enhanced on a daily basis over a period of years and decades, long into old age. Health is not a statistical average, but a potentiated norm; the highest possible individual accomplishment. It is willpower in visible form, a lasting monument to the strength of our will. Health is the optimisation of the individual for the optimal social good. Health is what we naturally desire for ourselves and is therefore the natural objective of society, politics and law. If we cease to strive for health, we are not at risk of illness, we are already ill.

Foreword to Heinrich Kramer, *Health as the Principle of State Legitimacy*, Berlin/Munich/Stuttgart, 25th edition

The Judgment

In the name of THE METHOD

Judgment in the case of Mia Holl, German national and biologist

1. The Charge
The Defendant was charged with anti-Method activities.

2. Composition of the Court
Judgment was given in a public sitting of the second penal chamber of the criminal court, composed as follows:

− Dr Ernest Hutschneider, chairperson and presiding judge
− Dr Hager and Frau Stock, associate judges
− Lay judges:
    Irmgard Gehling, housewife
    Max Maring, businessman
− Dr Barker, public prosecutor
− Dr Lutz Rosentreter, defence counsel
− Herr Danner, clerk of the court

3. Decision of the Court

i. The Defendant has been found guilty of anti-Method activities on the following counts: orchestrating a terrorist campaign, conspiring to cause civil unrest, unauthorised use of toxic substances and non-participation in compulsory testing to the detriment of the general good.

ii. The Defendant is sentenced to freezing for an unlimited term.

iii. The Defendant is ordered to pay court fees and all associated costs.

4. Background to the Case

The court's decision was based on the following facts:

Midday, Mid-Century

The hills form a tree-lined ring around towns that have grown into each other. Transmitters reach up to the clouds, where fleecy undersides are no longer grey with the foul breath of a civilisation that marked its presence on the planet by expelling filth on an epic scale. A few wide-eyed lakes with long, reedy lashes gaze up at the sky – gravel pits and quarries, now abandoned and flooded. Not far from the lakes, disused factories are home to community centres. A stretch of abandoned motorway and some abandoned churches with belfries are the main attractions of a scenic but seldom visited open-air museum.

These days nothing stinks here. Nothing is mined, drilled, burnt or covered in soot; the people here have found peace, have stopped fighting nature and stopped fighting themselves. White houses, small and box-like, are scattered across the hillsides; here and there they join together in rows, lining the slopes like tiers of an apartment block. A vista of flat roofs fills the horizon, mirroring the blue of the sky – a frozen ocean stretching endlessly into the distance, solar panels by the million, an almost unbroken expanse.

Magnetic train tracks cut long metallic pathways through the woods, heading straight for the middle of the glassy ocean of roofs. This is where our story begins, in the middle of the city, in the middle of the day, in the middle of the twenty-first century.

Beneath one of these roofs, longer and wider than most, Justitia is going about her usual business. Room 20/12, the room for conciliation hearings F–H, is maintained at a steady 19.5 degrees – the temperature at which humans think best. Sophie never comes to work without her cardigan, which in criminal hearings she wears beneath her robes. By her right hand are the files from the morning's session; by her left, a smaller stack of cases is waiting to be heard. With her blonde hair and high ponytail, Sophie looks like the eager student she once was. She chews on a pencil and studies the image on the wall. Noticing that the counsel representing the public interest is looking at her, she removes the pencil from her mouth. Eight years ago, when she and Barker were at law school together, he used to drone on incessantly about the dangers of placing germ-riddled objects near the mouth. Not that anyone was likely to find a germ in a civic building.

A short distance away, Barker faces her, his files distributed across the desk, leaving a small corner for the private counsel to stack his notes. To signal their unity of purpose, the defenders of the public and private interest share a desk – in practical terms, an uncomfortable arrangement, but a worthy legal tradition all the same. Barker raises his right index finger and a new image is projected onto the wall. The picture shows a man in his twenties.

'A trivial offence,' says Sophie. 'Any previous charges or convictions?'

Rosentreter, the private counsel, is a nice young chap. When nervous, he has a habit of pulling out his hair and dropping it quietly to the floor. 'Nothing,' he assures her.

'An isolated case of excessive blood caffeine levels,' says Sophie. 'A written warning and no further action. Are we agreed?'

'Absolutely.' Rosentreter turns and looks expectantly at the public counsel, who nods. Sophie transfers a file from the left to the right.

'Well, folks,' says Barker. 'I'm afraid the next case isn't quite so easy. You're not going to like it, Sophie.'

'Is there a child involved?'

Barker raises his index finger and the image changes again, this time to show a middle-aged man. Full body shots, naked. Front and back. Inside and out. X-rays, ultrasounds and an MRI of the brain.

'You're looking at the father,' says Barker. 'Multiple prior convictions for abuse of toxic substances, primarily nicotine and ethanol. This time he's up for violating the laws on early detection of disease in infants and children.'

'How old is the little one?'

'Eighteen months. Female. Non-attendance at stages G2 plus G5 through to G7 of the compulsory medicals. More seriously, the father didn't bring her for screening – cerebral condition unknown and no information on allergies.'

'Very remiss. Couldn't someone have acted earlier?'

'The civic doctor did his best to remind the respondent

of his legal obligations, but the situation couldn't be resolved. In the end, a counsellor was appointed – not a moment too soon, I'm afraid. He found the child in a terrible state: undernourished with a serious case of diarrhoea and vomiting . . . She was lying in her own filth. Another few days, and it would have been too late.'

'How awful. Surely he knows a baby can't look after itself?'

'There were problems at home,' explains Rosentreter. 'He's a single parent—'

'We're aware of the circumstances, but to treat your own daughter with such . . .'

Rosentreter raises a weary hand to signal his agreement with Sophie. The gesture is barely over when the door behind him opens. The new arrival doesn't knock or apologise for the disturbance: he moves with the confidence of a man accustomed to going where he pleases. His suit is perfectly tailored and worn with the carefully measured insouciance that true elegance requires. His hair is dark, his eyes are almost black, and his limbs are long but not lanky. He has the deceptive ease of a predator – a big cat with its eyes half closed, but ready to attack at any time. Only those who know Heinrich Kramer would notice the tremor in his fingers, which he disguises by keeping his hands in his trouser pockets. When outdoors, he wears a pair of white gloves, which he now removes.

'Santé, one and all!' He places his briefcase on a spare table and pulls up a chair.

'Santé, Herr Kramer!' says Barker. 'Still on the hunt for a good story?'

'The fourth estate never sleeps.'

Barker laughs for a second, stopping only when he realises that Kramer isn't joking.

Kramer leans forward with a frown, staring intently at the private counsel as if to remember who he is. 'Santé, Rosentreter,' he says, inflecting every syllable.

Rosentreter looks up briefly and buries his head in his files. Kramer straightens the crease of his trousers, crosses his legs, tilts his head, and cultivates the look of a casual observer, a difficult role for a man like him.

'Back to the case,' says Sophie briskly. 'Let's hear the recommendations from the public advocate.'

'Three years.'

'Isn't that overly harsh?' objects Rosentreter.

'Not in my opinion,' says Barker. 'The fellow needs to realise he endangered his daughter's life.'

'I suggest a compromise,' intervenes Sophie. 'Two years of correctional measures to be undertaken at home. In addition, appointment of a medical guardian for the little one and compulsory attendance at medical and hygiene classes for the father. That way the child will be safe and the family will get another chance. What do you think?'

'Exactly what I was going to suggest,' says Rosentreter.

'Marvellous.' Sophie smiles and turns to Barker. 'Can you justify your original recommendation?'

'The father's failure to fulfil basic sanitary and medical requirements was detrimental to the child's well-being,' says Barker. 'Parents have rights, but that doesn't include the right to endanger their offspring. Legally, there's no difference between deliberately exposing a child to danger and inflicting actual injury. In other circumstances we'd be talking grievous bodily harm.'

Sophie makes a note. 'Agreed,' she says, placing the file to the right. 'Let's hope the matter has been resolved in everyone's best interest.'

Kramer uncrosses and recrosses his legs before settling back down.

'Next case,' says Barker, raising an index finger. 'Mia Holl.'

The woman on the screen could be as young as twenty or as old as forty. Her date of birth puts her somewhere in the middle, a predictable place for the truth to be found. Her face glows with a special aura of cleanliness, which we also detect on the other faces in the room; it imparts a sense of innocence, of agelessness – an almost childlike air. It is the look of human beings who have never felt pain. Mia seeks our gaze trustingly. Her naked body is slight, but her physique is wiry and resilient. Kramer sits upright.

'Another petty offence.' Sophie glances at the topmost file and barely suppresses a yawn.

'What was her name again?' The question comes from Kramer. Although the words are spoken softly, everyone stops at the sound of his voice. Surprised, lawyers and judge look up from their files.

'Mia Holl,' says Sophie.

With a leisurely gesture, as if to bat away a fly, Kramer signals for the hearing to continue. With his other hand, he pulls a digital notebook from his trouser pocket and starts to take notes. Sophie and Rosentreter exchange glances.

'What have we got?' asks Sophie.

'Violation of duty to provide medical data,' says Barker. 'Nutritional records and sleep patterns overdue for the current month. Sudden cessation of sporting activity. Failure to provide home blood pressure readings and urine samples.'

'What of her general stats?'

At Barker's command, long lists of numbers appear on the wall: blood values, energy expenditure, metabolic rate, plus graphs recording physical performance.

'She looks well enough to me,' says Sophie, giving Rosentreter his cue.

'No prior offences. A successful biologist with an exemplary CV. No signs of physical impairment or social disability.'

'Has she availed herself of the Central Partnership Agency?'

'They haven't received her application yet.'

'It's obviously an aberration, isn't it, chaps?' says Sophie. She laughs at the lawyers' faces: Barker, disgruntled, and Rosentreter, shocked. 'I'd rather not issue an official caution,' she continues. 'Mediation seems appropriate. We'll invite her to see us.'

'Whatever you think,' says Barker with a shrug.

'An aberration?' Kramer smiles and taps his handheld display. 'That's one way of putting it.'

'Are you acquainted with the respondent?' enquires Sophie in a friendly tone.

'The judge's discretion is admirable.' Kramer's eyes twinkle at her, full of charming scorn. 'You've also met the respondent, Sophie, even though under different circumstances.'

Sophie thinks for a moment. If it weren't for her naturally ruddy complexion, it would be obvious she is blushing. Kramer returns his digital notebook to his pocket and gets up to leave.

'Finished already?' asks Barker.

'Far from it; I'm just getting started.'

With a brief wave, Kramer leaves the room, while Sophie closes the file and reaches for the stack to her left.

'Next, please.'

Pepper

'I'm telling you: it came from the nursery. Like this . . .'
Lizzie lets go of the stair rail, swoops forward dramatically and simulates a sneeze. 'Achoo!'

'Are you sure?' Pollie glances around nervously as if a ghost were ascending the stairs. 'You mean someone was actually . . . ?'

'Go on, say it!'

'Someone was sneezing?'

'Exactly! It came from the nursery; I was there in a flash!'

'Sneezing? What nonsense!' Completing the trio is Driss: tall, slender and without curves, like a sapling. Her flat face rests moonlike on the collar of her white tabard, her big eyes are mirrors, reflecting the others' gaze. Even without her freckles she would look younger than her years.

'Why is it nonsense?' asks Pollie.

'The common cold was eradicated in the twenties,' says Driss.

'Thank you, Fräulein Lightning.' Lizzie rolls her eyes.

'There was a warning just recently,' murmurs Pollie.

'Did you hear that, Driss? Pollie reads *The Healthy*

Mind. So here's me, with my heart in my throat, standing in the doorway, and what do I see? Ute's little lad crouching next to my poppet, who's got her nose in a bag of pepper – sneezing for all she's worth!'

Pollie starts to laugh. 'Goodness,' she says, 'they were *playing*!'

'She was pretending to be sick!' says Driss, joining in.

'Honestly, I could have done with a doctor myself, they gave me such a fright.'

The three women are standing in the hallway, as if to recreate the constellation of the previous day – and the day before that, and every other day. The eternal chain of recurrence reaches forward as well as back, offering the exact same picture for days and weeks to come: Lizzie, propped against the coiled hose of the disinfection machine, Pollie resting on the bacteriometer, and Driss with both arms on the stair rail. The main door opens, and the women stop talking at once. It's him again: the man in the dark suit. The lower half of his face is obscured by a white cloth, but anyone can see from his eyes that he is dashingly handsome.

'Santé! Good afternoon, ladies!'

'I've seen better,' says Lizzie, sticking out a hip and resting a hand on her waist. 'A really good afternoon is when there's nothing for us to do.'

Driss points to the man's face. 'You know you don't have to . . . ?'

'She means you don't need a hygiene mask,' says Pollie quickly.

'This is a monitored house,' explains Lizzie. 'You won't catch anything here.'

'Ah, the plaque by the door!' Kramer loosens the band at the back of his head. 'I should have realised.'

He stuffs the mask into his jacket pocket. Silence ensues.

Since no one is likely to speak for some time, we may as well go over some facts with regard to monitored housing. Certain households, selected for their reliability, have the privilege of carrying out prophylactic measures otherwise performed by the hygiene board. Duties include regular monitoring of air quality, testing of household waste and sewage, and disinfection of all areas accessible to the public. Monitored buildings are identified by a plaque outside the front door and residents are entitled to cut-price water and power. The initiative has exceeded expectations on all fronts: not only does the state save money on public health, but individuals learn the value of community spirit. In the dark and distant past, it was claimed that people were too stupid or lazy to pool their resources and contribute democratically to public life; this view has been discredited. The residents of monitored houses are living proof that humans are absolutely capable of working together for the common good; in fact, they enjoy it. It gives them a chance to meet up, talk and make decisions: to have something *to do* with each other for a change.

The man before us is positioned among the trio of white tabards with the pride of a stallion among goats. Heinrich Kramer was instrumental in introducing the monitored housing scheme, but he was famous beforehand. There isn't a person in the country who doesn't know who he is. This is the reason for the protracted silence and the explosion of chatter.

'Holy dirt, if it isn't . . .'

'Well, I'll be . . .'

'Is it really *you*?'

'For pity's sake, Driss, stop staring!'

Kramer places a hand on his chest and bows. 'The pleasure is mine, ladies. Perhaps you can direct me to Frau Mia Holl?'

'Mia!' squeals Driss, clapping her hands. If anyone had asked her which of her neighbours might receive a visit from Heinrich Kramer, she would have picked Mia Holl. Not for any reason – she just thinks Mia is special, that's all. 'She lives on the top floor: the apartment with the balcony to the rear.'

'It's a nice pad,' adds Pollie. 'I wouldn't mind being a scientist myself.'

'She does a difficult job,' says Lizzie reprovingly.

'I don't doubt it,' says Kramer. 'Is she in?'

'She's always in,' says Driss. 'Well, at the moment, at least.' She moves closer as if to impart a secret. 'We hardly see her any more.'

'What Driss means,' Lizzie corrects her, 'is that Frau Holl is taking a break from work.'

'Ah, a holiday . . .'

'Hardly,' snorts Pollie. 'Such a pretty girl and always up there by herself. The poor thing is trawling through possible matches.'

'We think Frau Holl is looking for a partner,' explains Lizzie knowingly.

Kramer nods. 'Thank you, ladies. Now if you'll excuse me.'

'Mia's a decent person.'

'Herr Kramer never thought otherwise. Honestly, Driss!'

'This is a monitored house, remember!'

'Thank you, ladies,' says Kramer, exiting the circle. He nods to each in turn. 'You've been most helpful. And congratulations on your impeccable house.'

Their mouths are open but no one says anything as Kramer, long legs and elastic body, disappears up the stairs.

The Ideal Inamorata

'Since life,' says Mia, 'is meaningless and yet you have to keep going, I sometimes feel like making sculptures out of copper pipes. I could weld them together and make a crane, or pile them up randomly like a nest of fossilised worms. Afterwards, I'd put them on a plinth and give them a name: "Temporary Structures" or "The Ideal Inamorata".'

Mia is sitting at her desk with her back to the room; from time to time she jots something down on one of the sheets of paper in front of her. Meanwhile, the ideal inamorata is reclining on the couch, clad in her beautiful hair and the light of the afternoon sun. We don't know if she understands what Mia is saying or even if she can hear her voice because she doesn't show any sign of listening or understanding. For all we know, the ideal inamorata may live in another dimension that borders on Mia's world. Her gaze, as she stares into space, resembles the lidless stare of a fish.

'I'd like to make something that will last,' says Mia. 'Something useless. Things with a purpose become redundant once their purpose is fulfilled. God's purpose was to give us solace, and look what happened to him! So much for his being immortal. Am I making any sense?'

The room is a mess. It looks as though no one has cleaned, tidied or aired the apartment for weeks.

'Of course you know what I'm talking about; I was quoting Moritz. "Anyone interested in the eternal must abandon all notion of purpose, including the purpose of one's continued presence on this earth," he used to say.'

When the ideal inamorata says nothing, Mia swivels round in her chair. 'An artist, that's what he said I should be. He was trying to provoke me. In his view, I was corrupted by science. How can you look at an object, let alone a person you love, if at the same time you're thinking that everything – the viewer and the viewed, the world and everything in it – is just a mass of spinning atoms? How can you cope with knowing that the brain, our only way of seeing and understanding, is made of the same basic material as everything we see and know? What are we left with? A world of matter staring at itself. That's how he put it.'

The ideal inamorata's relationship to matter is tenuous, which might be why Mia enjoys their conversations. She carries on talking without waiting for a response. 'Science,' she says, 'destroyed the divine and shifted humankind to the heart of the action. It left us stranded without any answers in a position that's patently absurd. Moritz said so all the time, and he was right. He and I had the same way of thinking; our conclusions were different, that's all.'

Mia points her pen at the ideal inamorata as if to accuse her of an unspecified crime.

'He wanted to live his life for love. From the way he said it, love was just a word for anything he liked: love was nature, freedom, women, catching fish, hellraising. Being different. Hellraising. That's what he meant by love.'

Mia turns back to her desk and continues to talk while noting things down.

'I need to write it down. I need to write *him* down. Ninety-six per cent of information is deleted from our memories after only a couple of days. Four per cent isn't enough for Moritz. If all I have is four per cent of Moritz, I can't carry on.'

She writes furiously for a moment, then she lifts her head.

'When we talked about love, he used to be very rude. You're a scientist, he would say. He accused me of putting everyone – friends and enemies – under an electron microscope. Tell me, Mia, when you say the word *love*, does the word feel foreign in your mouth? Because your voice sounds different when you say it. You're half an octave higher. Your larynx is constricting and your voice sounds shrill. *Love*. When you were little, you practised saying it in front of the mirror. *Love*. You used to look yourself in the eye and ask yourself why it took such an effort to say. *Love*. The fact is, Mia, you can't pronounce it properly. For you, it belongs to a foreign language, you have to contort your tongue. Go on, Mia, say I *love* you. Say, *love* is more important than anything. Say, my *love*, my *beloved*. Do you *love* me? – Mia, you're giving up already! Don't walk away!'

She swivels round in her chair, this time impatiently.

'What were his last words? "Life is an offer you can also refuse." Where's the love in that? Sometimes a sentence cuts into the mind like a machine press, changing the template of your thoughts. How am I supposed to forget? How am I supposed to remember? You knew him, probably better than I did. I have no idea if he knew how much I loved him! I don't even know if I miss him enough!'

'That's rubbish,' says the ideal inamorata. 'We're missing him right now; day and night, all we do is miss him. We miss him together. Now come here!'

Mia gets up and walks towards the outstretched arms of the ideal inamorata. Just then, the doorbell rings.

A Nice Gesture

There are moments when time seems to stop. Two human beings look into each other's eyes: matter staring at itself. For a few seconds the whole world seems to spin around the axis of their gaze, which passes through both skulls, extending to infinity. To avoid any possible confusion, let it be noted: we are not talking about love at first sight here. If we were to describe what is currently occurring between Mia and Kramer, we might compare it to the silent roar of a story about to unfold.

Mia has opened the door, and for a moment no one says a word. It is hard to guess what Kramer is thinking; possibly he is waiting for Mia to remember her manners and invite him inside. He is a patient man. In all likelihood, he is trying not to rush her, waiting respectfully in the doorway to give her time because he understands her present situation is unusual. She is face to face with the person whom she has killed in her imagination in multiple and agonising ways. It isn't the sort of thing that happens all the time.

'How odd,' says Mia when she finally finds her voice. 'The television isn't on and I can still see you quite clearly.'

Kramer responds with a charming, open-hearted smile,

a smile that no one who knows his media personality would ever believe was his. It is a private smile. A smile that says, despite his celebrity, he is still the same person at heart.

'Santé,' he says, removing his right glove and offering Mia his bare hand. She considers it closely, as if examining an exotic insect, then places her fingers in his.

'A nice gesture,' she says. 'Straight from an old movie. It seems incongruous somehow. Aren't you afraid of infection?'

'Nothing is more important in life than style, Frau Holl – and hysteria is the enemy of stylishness.'

'I suppose your face is like a label,' says Mia pensively. 'You can stick it on whatever opinion you like.'

'May I come in?'

'Surely you're not asking me to welcome my brother's murderer into my home?'

'I wouldn't insult your intelligence with such a melodramatic question. But you could offer me a drink . . . Perhaps some hot water?'

Kramer strolls past Mia and heads for the sofa, causing the ideal inamorata to roll hastily aside. As soon as Kramer sits, the sofa seems made especially for him. He is untroubled by the look of revulsion on the ideal inamorata's face – not because he doesn't care what she thinks, which he probably doesn't, but because he can't see her.

'Just to set things straight; I'm not the one who killed your brother. We could ask ourselves how he came by the fishing twine to hang himself in his cell.'

Mia stops in the middle of the room, hugging her body. Her fingernails press into her flesh; she seems to be clinging to herself as if she is scared of falling. Or perhaps she is worried that her hands will break away and throttle Heinrich Kramer.

'So,' she says hoarsely, 'I guess you're not here to persuade me not to hate you.'

Kramer smiles a flattered smile and smooths his hair. 'Please,' he says, 'be my guest: hate away! I came to talk to you, not to marry you.'

'I'd like to think we're immunologically incompatible.'

'Interestingly enough,' says Kramer, stroking his nose, 'we're a match.'

'Interestingly enough,' says the ideal inamorata, stroking her nose sarcastically, 'you're an even bigger arsehole than we thought.'

'Let's look at this logically.' Mia's voice has returned to normal. 'If you and your pack of yapping dogs hadn't waged that campaign against Moritz, the verdict might have been different. And if the verdict had been different, he probably wouldn't have taken his life.'

'Excellent, Frau Holl, I prefer you like this.' Kramer is resting his right arm on the back of the couch as if to embrace the ideal inamorata. 'Like me, you're a logical thinker, so you'll notice the error in your reasoning. Causality isn't the same as guilt. If it were, the Big Bang would be responsible for your brother's death.'

'Who says it wasn't?' says Mia, swaying as the Earth hits a pothole. She staggers, clutches at her desk and finds nothing but empty space. 'Do you want my verdict? The Big Bang: guilty. The universe: guilty. My parents who brought us into this world: guilty. Everything and everyone who caused his death: guilty.'

'Come on, Frau Holl, let me help you.' Kramer leaves the sofa and crouches next to Mia, who has sunk to her knees. He guides her to the sofa and smooths a strand of hair gently from her forehead.

'Get your hands off her,' hisses the ideal inamorata.

'I think we both need a cup of hot water,' says Kramer, heading for the kitchen.

Genetic Fingerprint

The incident under discussion took place in the recent past. If we consider what happened, the chain of events seems strikingly clear. On an otherwise ordinary Saturday evening, twenty-seven-year-old Moritz Holl, a warm-hearted but strong-willed young man, described as a 'dreamer' by his parents, a 'free spirit' by his friends and a 'bit of a nutcase' by his sister Mia, made a terrible discovery and went to the police. A young woman by the name of Sibylle, who was meeting Moritz on a so-called 'blind date' beneath the South Bridge, was at the time of his arrival neither interesting nor uninteresting, but dead. The distraught young man reported the incident, gave his particulars and left. Two days later he was placed in police custody. Traces of his semen had been discovered in the body of the deceased.

The matching of Moritz's DNA made further investigation unnecessary. No one with any sense would dispute the fact that DNA fingerprints are unique. Even twins aren't necessarily genetically identical, and Moritz's only sibling isn't a twin, but a scientist, who knows with good reason that a person's genetic fingerprint is unique. In murder cases with clear DNA evidence, there is never any uncertainty about the outcome of the trial, nor about whether the murderer will confess. Whether as a means of salving the conscience or asking popular opinion for absolution for a crime, sooner or later a proven killer always confesses. Moritz, however, seemed ignorant of this fact. He insisted that he had neither raped nor killed Sibylle. As the public sat down to watch the afternoon's entertainment in expectation of a speedy trial, Moritz, his pale face hardened by the strength of his convictions and his blue eyes wide with innocence, proceeded to claim that he wasn't guilty of the crime. Whenever he was permitted to speak, he said something that stuck in people's minds like a rock anthem: 'You are sacrificing me on the altar of your delusions.'

His attitude was unique in the Method's legal history. The citizens of a well-run state are aware that private interests must be aligned with the public good, especially in the murkier regions of human existence. Moritz's courtroom appearances caused a media scandal. The constancy of his stance impressed a number of people, who called for the judge to stay the sentence. Others found new cause to despise him: first for being a murderer, and second for being obtuse.

Amid all the excitement and confusion was Mia, her connection to Moritz now a dirty secret that the law was determined to conceal. By day she went to work and kept up with her exercise requirements; in the evening she visited the prison unobserved. Most nights, instead of sleeping, she vomited into a bowl and went outside to pour the contents down the drain: the slightest increase in stomach acid would be detected by the sensor in her toilet. Unsurprisingly, Kramer's reports played an important, if not decisive, role in shaping the media discourse on the case. What he wrote and said was what any right-thinking, dedicated defender of scientific positivism and the Method would say and write — and now, as he busies himself in the kitchen, he repeats it to Mia.

No High-flown Beliefs

'Our society,' says Kramer, filling the kettle, 'has attained its apotheosis. Unlike every previous or current form of social organisation, we're not in thrall to the market or religion. We're not dependent on high-flown ideological beliefs. The smug, self-serving faith in popular democracy has no place in our system. Our society is guided by reason and reason alone: its sole founding principle is taken directly from biological life. Every living organism has one thing in common, a defining characteristic that makes plants, animals and, most especially, humans what they are: the individual and collective will to survive. The consensus at the heart of our society is based on this unconditional drive, the cornerstone of our system. The Method was developed so that every individual can enjoy maximum longevity and minimal biological dysfunction – or put simply, a happy and healthy life, a life free from suffering and pain. With this in mind, we created a highly complex system, an apparatus more sophisticated than any form of government, present or past. Our laws form a delicate, perfectly attuned network, the nervous system of the state. Our system is flawless, with the inbuilt strength of the human body. And like the human body it is supremely capable of sustaining itself – but it is fragile too. The slightest infringement of the principles at the heart of this delicate organism could wound or kill it. Lemon?'

Mia, who likes a dash of lemon in her water, accepts the mug from Kramer. The hot water does her good. Kramer takes a seat in the armchair opposite her and blows into his cup.

'Do you see what I'm getting at?'

'The reliability of DNA data can't be contested in any rational way,' says Mia softly.

Kramer nods. 'DNA evidence is infallible. Infallibility is the bedrock of the Method. How are we supposed to explain the need for certain rules, if the rules themselves aren't unerringly rational and valid – or to put it another way, if they're fallible? Being infallible requires absolute consistency. It's simply good sense.'

'Listen to him, Mia,' says the ideal inamorata, 'he's talking in sound bites. The man is a machine!'

'Shush,' Mia tells her.

'Good sense,' continues the ideal inamorata, 'is knowing you're right without knowing why!'

'Stop butting in!'

'I beg your pardon?' says Kramer.

'Tell me,' says Mia, turning to face him. 'What does infallibility mean in human terms?'

'I can see where this is going.'

'How can you expect rules, regulations or procedures to be infallible when they're devised by humans? Humans change their beliefs, their scientific viewpoints, their entire notion of truth every couple of decades. Haven't you ever asked yourself whether, *in spite of everything*, my brother could have been innocent?'

'No,' says Kramer.

'Why not?' asks the ideal inamorata.

'Why not?' asks Mia.

'Let's take the question to its logical conclusion.' Kramer sets down his cup and leans towards her. 'What would we get? A legal system of exceptions and anomalies! The fickle rule of the heart, pardoning and punishing with the capriciousness of an absolute monarch. Whose heart should we use? Mine? Yours? With what claim to legality? Would we appeal to a higher authority? Do you believe in God, Frau Holl?'

'I don't believe in him and he doesn't believe in me. It's mutual.'

'What about Herr Kramer's system?' says the ideal inamorata. 'He doesn't believe in rational objectivity – and it doesn't believe in him!'

'And emotions?' counters Mia. 'They're hardly a reliable basis for decisions. By definition, they're merely personal.'

'Human reason is an illusion,' says the ideal inamorata. 'It's nothing but a vessel for the sum of your feelings.'

'Anachronistic, romantic claptrap,' snaps Mia.

'It didn't kill Moritz, though. Unlike your intellectual sophisms.'

'Frau Holl!' Kramer waves a shapely hand as if to dispel a cloud of mist. 'Please desist from talking to yourself. You've lost a brother, not your confidence in the system.'

'Which Moritz despised,' throws in the ideal inamorata.

Mia casts a warning look in her direction and walks to the window. It is a beautiful day, straight from a commercial for protein supplements. Mia fights back the urge to close the curtains. The sunlight reveals half-eaten takeaways, discarded items of clothing, and dust gathering in the corners. It reeks of the twentieth century. The bright light seems to magnify the chaos with every passing minute.

'From here I can see two paths,' says Mia. 'One is marked misery, the other ruin. I can curse a system founded on a Method to which there is no rational alternative; or I can betray my love for my brother, whose innocence seems as clear to me as the fact of my own existence. Do you see?' She swings around violently. 'I *know* he didn't do it. What course should I take: hell or damnation? Should I fall or should I fall?'

'Neither,' says Kramer. 'In certain situations, the error lies not in the choices you make, but in making a decision at all.'

'But . . . are you of all people telling me there are flaws in the system?'

'Of course.' His smile, which has never faded, becomes disarming. He looks up at her from the armchair. 'The system is human, you said so yourself. Inevitably it has its flaws. The human condition is a pitch-black room in which we crawl around like newborn babies, unseeing, unhearing. The best we can do is to avoid bumping heads. Nothing more.'

'Bumping heads? Mine is in pieces.'

'Not in my opinion; not from what I'm seeing right now.' Kramer extends an arm and points at the middle of Mia's forehead. 'You need to rise above all this. By all means, grieve for your brother; grieve all you like. But while you're grieving, go back to normal life. You've come to the attention of the authorities because of certain lapses.'

'In certain situations . . .' begins Mia, but Kramer is shaking his head.

'You don't need to justify yourself to me, Frau Holl. You'll be invited to a conciliation meeting by the court. Be sure to accept. And tidy up! Scrub the visible signs of despair from your life. It's still *your* life, remember. You need to assume control.'

'I fully intend to,' says Mia softly.

'I'm pleased to hear it.' Kramer leaps up energetically as if to take charge of the clean-up operation.

Mia eyes him dubiously. 'You'll need a bucket if you're going to scrub away the visible signs of my despair.'

Kramer immediately puts his hands in his pockets and changes his pose.

'Which leads me to an interesting question,' continues Mia. 'You're a busy man with no shortage of suitable people to talk to. Are you planning to adopt me?'

'In other words,' says the ideal inamorata, 'what the hell are you doing here?'

'I'm here,' says Kramer, 'to make a suggestion.' He strolls around the room, stopping briefly to check the computer on Mia's exercise bike which is displaying a line of zeros.

'Everything we've been discussing affects the whole country, not just you. It won't be long before the first journal articles are published – the case of Moritz Holl, as described by leading experts in sociology, psychology, politics and law. The incident will rise to become the queen of footnotes, referenced in every academic paper: Moritz Holl, the man who was proven guilty by the Method and pleaded innocent in the face of the evidence. How? Why? What led to the sudden disjunction between private interest and public good? These questions cut to the heart of our society; they're fundamental questions about the workings of the Method, questions we should never stop asking and discussing.'

Mia follows him around the room with her gaze. Her face shows astonishment.

'Asking? Discussing? Are you suggesting I . . . critique the system for your newspaper?'

'I'd like an in-depth conversation with you. I want to write about you, Mia. A profile piece for *The Healthy Mind*. Gone are the days when journalism was a travelling circus; we don't pack up and move on when the show is over.'

'Ha, that's a good one,' says the ideal inamorata. 'I'd laugh out loud if I could.'

'With your help, I could show that tragedies and contradictions are inevitable even in a well-ordered system like the Method. We could demonstrate why it still makes sense to follow the path of reason. A good citizen shouldn't follow the crowd like a sheep. A good citizen should work through periods of doubt and crisis to emerge a stronger supporter of the common cause. People would understand it, coming from you. Have a think about it, Frau Holl. It wouldn't do you any harm.'

'If you agree to it,' says the ideal inamorata, 'I'm leaving you.'

'You can't,' says Mia. 'You're a present from Moritz.'

Kramer stiffens. 'You're starting to frighten me, Frau Holl.'

Through Plexiglas

'That's another thing I wish we'd done,' says Mia.

If we peer through time as if it were a gauzy robe veiling the body of the Eternal, we see Mia and Moritz in a bare room at the remand centre, four weeks ago at most. They are looking at each other attentively, as if seeing each other for the first time.

'Namely?' asks Moritz.

'I wish we'd had time to find you a woman.'

They are separated by a wall of Plexiglas, at the centre of which is a star-shaped constellation of small holes. Through these holes Moritz and Mia can talk to each other; if they move a little closer, close enough to anger the guard, they can even smell each other.

'It's all right,' says past-tense Moritz, 'I invented one instead.'

'One what?'

'An ideal inamorata. She can be a bit moody, but most of the time we get along fine. I'm not lonely.'

When Moritz moves, his white paper suit, which has replaced his clothes for the past six months, starts to rustle. He presses two fingers against the screen; Mia does the same on the other side. This time they get away with it: Mia is supplying the guard with sachets of illicit caffeine powder from the lab. She and Moritz look at each other and smile. They have learned to smile when really they want to scream, smash things or just cry.

'Tell you what,' says Moritz, 'you can borrow her. Take her home with you.'

'You want me to take home your imaginary lover?'

'It's a great idea. That way it will be easier to believe we'll see each other soon. The ideal inamorata will steer you back to me. She won't last long at your place, I bet.'

'You need a certain amount of imagination for a game like that.'

Moritz frowns just as he always frowns. It looks as if his whole face is trying to congregate around a point between his eyes. 'You've got plenty,' he says. 'Ever since we were little we've been meeting in the realm of imagination.'

'It was *your* realm.'

'It was *ours*; it *is* ours. It will always be *our* home; yours and mine. Remember that.'

For a moment they glare at each other like enemies, a pair of cowboys on a dusty road. The wind rushes past, blowing their hair in the same direction. They square off, a brief skirmish, then Mia feels herself give in. The truth is, she wasn't really trying in the first place.

'OK,' she says, 'I'll take your imaginary female if I must.'

His forehead smooths easily; the mind behind it is accustomed to getting its way. 'She'll be waiting in your apartment,' he whispers. 'She's my present to you; you'll learn to love her, you'll see. And now . . . I need a favour from you.'

In Mia's fingers is a clear plastic cord, which she feeds through a hole in the Plexiglas. With small movements of his thumb and index finger, Moritz pulls it through the screen. It takes time. The guard inspects his fingernails and yawns. When the cord has passed through the hole, Mia and Moritz stand up.

'Life,' says Moritz softly, 'is an offer you can also refuse.'

They imagine hugging each other, standing a tiny distance apart so their chests don't quite touch.

'So long,' says Mia.

A Special Gift for Pain

It isn't that she didn't try. She cleared the shelves and
surfaces of dirty dishes and empty glasses and stacked
them on her desk. She laid out the kit for her blood test
and placed the beaker for her urine sample on the toilet
cistern, where it remained, unused. She vacuumed a
corner of the carpet and threw the vacuum cleaner on
the floor. Rather than clean the windows, as she intended,
she dabbed star-like constellations of dots on the steamed-
up glass. Afterwards, she pressed on the dots with two
fingers and smiled when actually she wanted to scream,
smash things, or just cry. Now the apartment is messier
than before and Mia is lying on the sofa in the arms of
the ideal inamorata. Her eyes are closed as if she were
asleep.

'I don't recognise my apartment any more,' says Mia.
'It looks strange, like a word repeated and repeated until
it's just a series of sounds. Time seems strange to me, the
passing of days. I don't recognise my life any more; it's
just a set of actions. No meaning, no purpose.'

'This Kramer is a fanatic,' says the ideal inamorata,
cradling Mia like a child.

'I'm a woman with a penthouse apartment overlooking

the city and a special gift for pain. I haven't been outside in four weeks. That's the sum of my life. If I turn my gaze inwards, if I listen for signs of activity, a rustling, a whispering, the slightest stirring of a personality, I find nothing. I'm a word that's lost its meaning because it's been repeated to death.'

'He gets a kick out of absolute obedience,' says the ideal inamorata. 'Unquestioning sacrifice to the principle, that's what he wants.'

'He talked a lot of sense.'

'He's a *clever* fanatic.' The ideal inamorata lifts her arms above her head and holds her wrists together, shaking her hands in the air as if to recall a bathing bird. This is how the ideal inamorata laughs.

Tin of Beans

She was brought in by two guards in grey uniforms, who apologised politely for the inconvenience and closed the door gently on their way out.

Now Mia, naked from the waist up, is in the examination chair. Her eyes are empty and expressionless. Wires run from her wrists, back and temples. The beating of her heart, the rush of blood through her body, the electrical impulses running through her synapses are clearly audible – an orchestra of demented musicians tuning their instruments. The civic doctor is a good-natured man with manicured fingernails. He passes a sensor over Mia's upper arm as if he were scanning a tin of beans at the checkout. Her picture appears on the wall, accompanied by a long list of medical stats.

'What did I tell you, Frau Holl? You're in perfect working order. Tiptop condition, as I like to say.'

Mia looks up at him.

'You thought I was ill? That I was holding back my data because I had something to hide . . . Do I look like a criminal?'

The doctor is already removing the wires.

'It wouldn't be the first time, Frau Holl. True, but sad, as I like to say.'

Mia pulls her jumper quickly over her head.

'You have a nice day, Frau Holl,' the doctor calls after her.

An Ordinary Juicer

Sophie's student ponytail bounces merrily back and forth as she scans the medical data on her desk. For no particular reason, she is in a good mood. For Sophie, good moods are a habit, just as people of more nervous dispositions are inclined to bite their nails. Sophie studied law because she loves it, and her love of law became a profession, a career that allows her to do something worthwhile. People thank her for it. *Most* people thank her for it. And Mia Holl, Sophie can tell at a glance, is definitely one of those people. As soon as Mia walked into the room, her bright eyes and intelligent face struck Sophie. Mia's nose is possibly too large for her face. Large noses are a sign of obstinacy, which in this case is balanced out by a soft mouth, pleading silently for harmony. Sophie is an excellent judge of character, she thinks.

'Very good,' she says, closing the medical dossier and pushing it aside. 'Excellent, in fact.'

Sophie is touched by the way the respondent is chewing her lower lip. Mia Holl, though several years older than Sophie, has the air of a helpless child.

'I'm delighted you're here, Frau Holl, although I wish you hadn't declined our offer of mediation. This is an official civil hearing and I must remind you of your rights. According to Article 50 of the Health Code, you have the right to remain silent – although I'm sure you'd rather talk to me. Isn't that right, Frau Holl?'

On occasions, Sophie can look like a child as well, a child who wants everyone to kiss and make up. Faced with this look, defendants have no choice but to nod.

Mia nods.

'Good,' says Sophie, smiling. 'Then tell us, Frau Holl, what do you understand by the concept of health?'

'Humans,' says Mia, apparently to her fingers, 'are surprisingly badly constructed. An ordinary juicer, for example, can be dismantled and taken apart. Unlike the components of a human, a juicer's parts can be cleaned, repaired and put back together.'

'In that case, you'll understand why our prophylactic measures for public health are designed for humans, not juicers.'

'Yes, Your Honour.'

'So why is it you've been exempting yourself from mandatory testing? You haven't returned a single sample in weeks.'

'I'm sorry,' says Mia. 'I guess.'

'You guess?' Sophie leans back and flips her ponytail into place. 'Frau Holl, I don't suppose you remember me, but I remember you very well. I was the rapporteur in the case against . . . uh, in the trial of Moritz Holl. The details of the affair are known to me. I understand what you're going through.'

Several seconds pass as Mia stares fixedly into the judge's eyes, then she lowers her gaze.

'We can't change what happened,' says Sophie, 'but the Health Code offers a number of solutions for people in your situation. I could appoint a medical counsellor to help you – or order a stay at a health farm, if you prefer. We could choose a nice spot in the mountains or by the sea. You'll have all the support you need to come to terms with your situation. When it comes to your reintegration into normal—'

'No, thank you.'

'What do you mean – no, thank you?'

Mia says nothing.

Sophie is mistaken in thinking that the respondent can't remember her. Mia's memory shows Sophie as a giant black-robed mannequin at the back of a ghost train, sheltered from the wind by the mannequins in front. Seated behind the presiding judge, the associate judges and the clerks, Sophie is barely visible: pretty, young, her blonde hair in a ponytail, the ultimate phantasm of horror, looking down with her big eyes and solicitous expression at the defendant, his body shrunken from its former size, a gaunt figure cowering in front of the black-robed brigade. The blonde girl's all right, Moritz had said. She doesn't mean any harm. Probably none of them do. How would you decide the case, *you* with *your* principles, if you were sitting up there and I weren't your brother?

'Frau Holl,' says Sophie, crinkling her cute little nose, 'in organic terms, you are perfectly healthy, but your soul is distressed. Would you agree with this assessment?'

'Yes.'

'Then why refuse our help?'

'My pain is a personal matter.'

'A personal matter?' echoes Sophie, surprised.

'It's like this.' Mia reaches suddenly for the judge's hand, a clear violation of courtroom procedure. Sophie sits up with a start and glances about, before allowing the defendant to grip her fingers.

'No one,' says Mia, 'no one understands what I'm going through, not even me. If I were a dog, I'd growl at myself to keep me at bay.'

Not Made to Be Understood

Mia's voice is barely a whisper because she realises that statements about growling dogs aren't made to be understood. What she wants to say isn't easy to put into words, and in the presence of a judge, it's probably good that she isn't inclined to try. If we were to find the words for her, we would have to imagine that it is night. Mia fights to free herself from her duvet and gets out of bed. Outside, the first rays of light are beginning to water down the thick nocturnal blackness of the sky. This is the time when yesterday becomes tomorrow and for the briefest of moments there is no today: this is the time that the sleepless dread. Mia is stuck in her skin. It traps her like a fishing net. Her face is too small: she runs her fingertips over an unfamiliar arrangement of features, her mouth in an ugly half-grin with only one side turned up − it isn't her smile.

She leaves the bedroom and her shoulder grazes the door frame. We see her cross the corridor and enter the lounge, pick up a remote control and turn on the stereo, racking up the volume. We don't hear her scream; we see her wide-open mouth and the way she stumbles, and we think she is going to fall. But Mia keeps going and reaches the window, her raised hands thudding against the pane. Knocked back, she takes another run-up and slams both palms against the window. Because of the music, we don't hear the noise of breaking glass. Carried by her momentum, Mia's arms pass through the shattering pane, and she snatches at nothing, tipping forward, then catching her balance before she hits the jagged edge of the frame. She grabs at the shards and clenches her fists, her eyes are closed and we see her lips tremble, her eyes looking up beneath their lids. We see her knuckles blanch and blood leaking out between her fingers as if she were crushing some-thing soft and red. Then she unclenches her fists, shakes her arms and fragments of glass fall to the ground. Blood streams past her elbows as she raises her hands and clasps them together. 'Take it away,' we read the words on her lips, 'take it away, won't you?' and she moans, as if the thing to be taken is unbearably heavy. Again and again she raises her hands beseechingly, and for a terrible moment we think she might actually be talking to us.

Imagine this: on this particular night and all the others like it, she doesn't fight her duvet, doesn't get up, doesn't run to the window, doesn't smash the glass, she just lies there, sleepless in the posture of someone sleeping – and now we start to get a sense of what she's going through.

Personal Matter

'Frau Holl,' says Sophie, passing the back of her hand over her face, 'I'm afraid you'll have to tell me what you mean by *personal matter*.'

Mia jumps to her feet and paces around the room as if searching for windows, of which there are none.

'I want to be left alone,' she says finally.

'Return to your seat, Frau Holl.'

'I'm not a schoolgirl any more. Certain things require time, and that's what I'm asking for – time to myself.'

'Frau Holl,' says Sophie sharply, 'you've committed a series of civil infractions, and now you're dangerously close to a criminal trial. Please sit down.'

Mia complies and the severity leaves the judge's features as quickly as it came. Briefly, so briefly it might be a trick of the memory, we caught a glimpse of an angry face.

'I'd like you to think about this carefully,' says Sophie. 'What would happen if you fell ill?'

'I'd see a doctor.'

'Who would pay for the doctor?'

'I . . . I can afford to pay.'

'And if you didn't have the means? Would society let you die?'

Mia is silent.

'Good sense dictates that society should look after your health in times of need,' says Sophie. 'By the same token, the onus is on you to ensure such circumstances don't arise. Do you see?'

'I wouldn't mind being ill,' says Mia stubbornly.

'Frau Holl,' exclaims Sophie, 'do you have any idea what you're talking about? Have you ever felt physical pain so intense you feared for your mental health? Do you know how dreadfully people suffered in the past? They watched themselves die by degrees and they called it *living*. Every step of the journey was a risk, a step towards perdition; a twinge in the chest, a tingle in the arm, and the end was in sight. People lived in constant fear of foundering on themselves; fear was *life* for these people. For humans to have risen above this condition is a blessing, don't you think?'

Mia is silent.

'I see you agree with me, Frau Holl. Avoiding all forms of illness is in your interest, and your personal interests coincide with those of the Method on this point. Oneness of purpose is the foundation of our system: there can be no room for personal matters when the general good and individual interests are connected in this way.'

'I know,' says Mia softly.

'You're not setting out to undermine the principles of the Method, then?'

'I'm a scientist, Your Honour. People in my profession know better than anyone that biological organisms seek to achieve well-being and avoid pain. Political systems are legitimate only if they serve these goals.' Mia wipes her palms on her trousers. 'I'm not trying to be difficult, Your Honour. I'm not myself any more, I'm probably talking nonsense, but I've always supported the Method.'

The conciliatory expression returns to Sophie's face. 'Exactly as I thought. Your final submission please.'

'I'd like to be left alone.'

'Are you sure?' Sophie opens the file with a sigh and picks up a pencil. 'I could refrain from prescribing auxiliary measures, I suppose.'

'That would be helpful.'

'On one condition,' says Sophie. She looks up, pencil poised. 'From now on you'll stay out of trouble.'

'I'll try.'

'No, Frau Holl. You will do more than try. This is an official warning. Give me your word.'

Mia raises an eyebrow, then raises her hand.

'There's no need to worry,' she says.

Pointed Horns: Part I

We're going to switch tenses for a while. Mia finds it painful to think of her brother in the past tense, but the rest of us will be fine.

'There's no need to worry,' said Moritz.

'You smell funny,' said Mia.

'I smell *good*. I smell human.'

'Your future partner might not think so.'

'Let me tell you a secret. So far my future partners have found me pretty hot.' He grabbed her hand. 'Come on.'

'Moritz! Can't you see?' she protested. 'The path ends *here*!'

'It always has done!'

There followed a tug of war, with Moritz grabbing Mia and dragging her along with both hands until she came of her own accord. Ducking under low-hanging branches, they tramped through the undergrowth. The path belonged to them. Beside the river was a little clearing shaded by trees. Moritz called it 'our cathedral'. A place of prayer, he liked to say. By prayer, he meant talking, saying nothing and fishing. Mia didn't approve of raising the stakes: she liked talking to her brother without it being a religion.

Moritz pulled some fishing line from his bag and snapped a branch from a tree. In no time he had sat down on the grass and cast his line; Mia was still unfolding a tissue to sit on. For a while they watched the water flowing by incessantly while the river remained exactly the same.

'Claudia?' enquired Mia.

'That was her name.'

'Well?'

'Lovely girl — an expert at deep-throating. You know what that is?'

Mia held up a hand to stop him. 'I don't want to know, thank you. You must be running out of immunologically compatible partners. How many have you got left?'

'Oh, 3.4 million or thereabouts. The Central Partnership Agency is the world's biggest brothel keeper — the crooked guardian of the gates to paradise.'

Still holding his makeshift fishing rod in one hand, Moritz stretched out his arms and put on a saccharine voice: 'Step forward, please. Major histocompatibility complex class B11. Slim hips, brown hair, twenty-four years of age, perfect health. Premium goods.'

'Who's next, then?'

'Kristine. An absolute dream girl.'

'Promise you'll take her seriously.'

'Doesn't it go without saying?' Moritz grinned. 'Seriousness is the first rule of pleasure. Anyway, how are you getting on with your sixteen-legged microbes?'

'Microbes don't have legs.' Mia poked him in the ribs. 'Actually, we're making good progress. Once I've—'

'Look out!'

Mia stiffened as her brother dropped his rod and grabbed her by the shoulders. There was rustling from the undergrowth on the opposite bank.

'Over there!' shouted Moritz in mock panic. 'A great big bacteria with pointed horns!'

'Don't be an idiot!' Mia laughed and wiped her brow. 'It was only a deer.'

'Precisely.'

'I don't suppose I'll ever understand what you want from life.'

'That reminds me . . . Want to hear something? It's especially for you.'

Moritz reached for his hygiene mask, which was hanging around his neck, and placed it on his head like an Alice band; then he picked up his rod.

'In my dreams,' he intoned, 'I see a city made for living, where the houses have rusty antennae like spiky hair. Where owls live in the beams of tumbledown attics. Where loud music and twisting ciphers of smoke rise from the upper floors of dilapidated factories, accompanied by the hearty clunking of billiard balls. Where every street lamp seems to shine on a prison yard. Where bicycles are parked in bushes and people drink wine from dirty glasses. Where young girls wear the same denim jacket and walk around hand in hand as though they're scared. Scared of other people. Scared of the city. Scared of life. Here, in this city, I run barefoot across building sites and watch the mud rising up between my toes.'

'Infantile and revolting,' said Mia. 'Whoever wrote it should be locked up.'

'Exactly what the judge thought,' said Moritz. 'Eight months for sedition.'

He hooked a cigarette out of his shirt pocket and pushed it between his lips. Mia's hand shot out and whisked it away.

'Where did you get hold of that?'

'Honestly, Mia,' said Moritz. 'Where do you think? I don't suppose you brought a light?'

Smoke

When Driss was little, she wanted to grow up like Mia. Now she is fully grown and sitting at the top of the stairs barely two paces from Mia's door, beneath which lies a mat, placed there as a tribute to a bygone age. Driss knows exactly where to sit in order to get the best view from the top-floor window. The apartment block is built on a slope, and the city lies at Driss's feet. It is an excellent place for dreaming. Most people don't come up this far, but Driss has brought a bucket and a bottle of disinfectant, just in case.

Her dreams unfold in two-dimensional Technicolor, like old-fashioned films. She usually casts Mia in the lead. Today, for example, she is watching Mia introduce herself to Kramer behind this very door. At first Driss doesn't really understand the conversation, despite Pollie's efforts to read to her regularly from *The Healthy Mind*. Kramer seems to be talking about the battle against the People's Right to Illness: he has chalked up some important victories in the anti-terrorist campaign. Lizzie's voice has a habit of rising half an octave when the PRI is in the headlines, but Mia listens quietly and asks a few questions. Kramer has never met anyone who understands him so well.

After a while, they fall silent. Driss likes to replay this moment in her head. She zooms in and watches at half-speed as Mia and Kramer, who are sitting side by side on the sofa, turn to each other slowly. They don't gaze into each other's eyes; each is focused on the other's mouth. Kramer puts an arm around Mia. If Driss were to do the same, her fingers would touch the white front door of Mia's apartment. She feels the hairs on her slender neck stand on end, she closes her eyes and holds her breath. In a moment, Kramer will lean forward and kiss Mia as people used to in movies when they didn't know about the risk of oral infection.

Driss feels a tingling in her nostrils. She opens her eyes and sniffs. There is a strange smell. She scans the landing and takes two more vigorous sniffs. No doubt about it: smoke. In an instant she is on her feet and racing down the stairs.

'Fire!' she shouts. 'Fire!'

At the end of the landing, behind the white door, Mia is lying on the sofa with the ideal inamorata, a cigarette between her lips and a blackened match on her thigh.

'This is it,' says Mia, taking a long drag on the cigarette, 'this is exactly how Moritz smelt.'

'You'd think he were here,' says the ideal inamorata, reaching out two fingers to take the cigarette.

No More Mediation

Dressed in her black robes, Sophie looks not unlike a nun without a veil. She has come to accept the likeness and knows it could be worse. At least when she puts the statute book under her bottom she no longer looks like a nun who's too small for her chair. The furniture in the court-room dates back to an era when judges were more stately. The problem is exacerbated by the ergonomic guidelines for workplace safety, which haven't been properly adhered to. On some days, admittedly few in number, Sophie hates her job.

Barker is thin and nervous today, as though his robe is concealing a bag of loose bones. The private counsel, this time in mufti, is alone in the public gallery, staring out of the window, apparently uninvolved. The clerk has got a new hairstyle — or maybe her grandma has come to the courtroom instead. She scans the defendant's arm: Mia's chip is in the same place as everyone else's, in the middle of the bicep, just beneath the skin. Sophie refreshes herself with oral disinfectant, ascertains the identity and presence of the various parties, and opens the hearing with the words: 'Is this your idea of a joke?'

'No, Your Honour,' says Mia, her face expressionless.

'Two days ago, you gave me your word. Do you remember what you promised?'

'Yes, Your Honour.'

'Do you know why you're here?'

'Abuse of toxic substances,' interrupts Barker for the prosecution. 'In contravention of Article 124 of the Health Code.'

Sophie places both hands on the lectern and leans forward as she fixes Mia with an angry glare. 'This isn't a conciliatory hearing,' she hisses. 'No discussion or mediation. You're a defendant, not a respondent. This, Frau Holl, is a criminal trial.'

This time Sophie's angry face appears for longer. It looks out of place with her ponytail.

Mia says nothing.

'What did we discuss two days ago?'

Mia still says nothing.

'Do you think I'm stupid? Is this a game to you? Answer me, Frau Holl!'

Mia tries to answer. She looks up, fills her lungs with air and opens her mouth. She would like to give the right answer, not least because she wants to please the nice judge. But the right answer won't come to her, and this is a terrible shock for Mia, as if she has suddenly realised that something fundamental about her life has changed. In Mia's world, it is customary for there to be an answer to each question or to be precise, *one* correct answer to every question. In Mia's world, a person's mind doesn't slosh like water around her head.

'Moritz,' she says, and the voice seems to come from somewhere else in the room, 'Moritz said smoking a cigarette is like journeying through time. It transported him to other places . . . places where he felt free.'

'The prosecution moves for the defendant's comments to be noted in her file,' says Barker.

'Rejected,' says Sophie. 'The defendant's statement shall be heard in full.'

'Forgive me, Your Honour,' says Barker with a special smirk: the same smirk he brought out for Sophie when he was arguing with her at law school, 'I was under the impression the court would be bound by the rules of criminal procedure.'

'Absolutely,' says Sophie, 'and in accordance with Article 12 of the Health Code, I will hold you in contempt if you interfere with my examination of Frau Holl.'

Barker presses his lips together as if there is something bitter in his mouth that good manners obliges him to swallow. Sophie massages the back of her neck and nods for Mia to continue.

'I feel the need to be close to him,' says Mia. 'As if death were a hedge that we could slip through with a bit of cunning. I still see Moritz, even though he's dead; I hear him, I talk to him. I spend more time with him than ever. I'm always thinking about him; I can't do anything without him. The cigarette tasted of Moritz: of his laughter, his zest for life, his need for freedom. And now I'm sitting here in front of you, exactly like him.' Mia laughs. 'We're closer than I ever thought.'

'Frau Holl,' says Sophie in a considerably calmer voice, 'I'm going to adjourn the proceedings and assign a counsel for your defence. After what you've said, I can't in all conscience allow you to continue. However, since you ignored my previous warning, your earlier infractions must be punished. What does the prosecution recommend?'

Taken unawares, Barker leafs through his notes and in his haste fails to find what he is looking for.

'Fifty days' wages,' he says at last.

'Twenty,' rules Sophie. 'The hearing is closed.'

Once the two black-robed mannequins have left the room, Mia is alone in the dock. In the public gallery behind her, the private counsel gets to his feet, steps forward and waits for Mia to turn round.

'Rosentreter,' he says. 'I'm your new lawyer.'

Nice Guy

He is clearly a nice guy. A little on the tall side and his fringe is a fraction too long: hardly a moment goes by without him pushing it away from his face. In fact, his fingers are constantly occupied, examining the contours of objects around him, checking his clothes are sitting properly, disappearing into his trouser pockets and emerging an instant later to clap an acquaintance on the shoulder – but his palm never touches the shoulder. Rosentreter's fingers are like a commando unit from the prophylactic health service, always on the go. At present they are engaged in a tactile examination of the tabletop, hence his stooped posture, which could otherwise be attributed to stomach cramps.

'I'm honoured,' he says. 'Truly honoured.'

'What's so honourable about a case like this?' Mia averts her gaze so as not to stare at his belt buckle. Rosentreter takes a step to the left, two steps to the right and decides to sit down. He manoeuvres the chair so he is facing the dock, where Mia is seated.

'First of all, my heartfelt condolences, Frau Holl. The last few months must have been hellish; you've coped admirably well.'

'If there were anything admirable about my coping, neither of us would be here.'

'Which,' Rosentreter says brightly, 'would be a shame.' He stops smiling when he notices that Mia, for good reason, doesn't share his point of view.

'All of this,' he says, starting afresh and indicating the courtroom with an expansive sweep of the hand, 'is just procedure. *Procedere*. A bureaucratic process set in motion by a particular type of action. It's like pressing a button. You mustn't take it personally.'

Mia watches as he unpacks his briefcase in search of a contract that will invest him with the authority to act in her defence. The hint of a smile crosses her face as he drops a sheath of pens.

'What did I tell you?' says Rosentreter, straightening up. His cheeks are bright red. 'The court system can't be that bad; not if people like me are allowed to work here. I knew your brother, by the way.'

Mia, about to sign her name, pauses.

'Really? Another pen-pusher in the army of mannequins—'

'I work for my clients!' Rosentreter's hands are flapping like startled birds. 'I'm the *private* counsel! It's my job to read the Method Defence bulletin for this jurisdiction every month. What more can I say?'

For a while he looks straight at Mia, as though he genuinely wants her to tell him what to say. He blinks a few times; his fringe is in his eyes.

Under normal circumstances, Mia would find him unbearable. He is precisely the sort of supposedly lovable clown who drives her up the wall. A man like Rosentreter keeps family photos in his wallet and shows them around in the supermarket queue. He is the sort of person who turns up late because he stops to help panicking strangers who are desperate not to turn up late. When asked about the meaning of life, he will make some crack about an ancient film. This is his idea of humour. To be honest, Mia only likes people with sharp minds and a willingness to put their intellect to the most effective use. She divides humanity into two categories: professional and unprofessional. Rosentreter very definitely belongs to the latter category. No amount of crying, screaming and waking in a cold sweat could be more revealing of Mia's present state than the fact that, despite everything, she is glad of his company. She feels herself relaxing with every breath.

'I never met Moritz in person,' says Rosentreter eventually. 'Only his virtual trace, if you know what I mean.'

'I'm not a lawyer. You'll have to speak plainly.'

'Of course, absolutely. It's very simple. Your brother was on the blacklist.'

'What does that mean?'

'Here and here,' says Rosentreter, pointing to the contract with his pen. Mia finally signs. 'He was under surveillance by Method Defence.'

'That's ridiculous. There must be some mistake. Moritz wasn't an enemy of the Method. That's . . .' Mia laughs. 'It's like pointing at a deer and seeing a great big bacteria with horns.'

'I'm sorry?'

'Never mind! Look, I'm willing to admit he was a bit of a child. He definitely had his own ideas. But he wasn't the type to join a group – especially not some shabby little protest movement.'

'Shabby little protest movement . . . of course not,' says Rosentreter in a soothing tone. 'I don't know why I mentioned it . . . Let's forget about it, Frau Holl! Just a few brief words on the legal technicalities, which, as your counsel, it's my duty to explain. When it comes to certain charges, our legal system can be somewhat oversensitive. If a defendant becomes implicated in anti-Method activities, it puts the case on a different footing, so to speak.' Right now, Rosentreter doesn't look like an oversized boy; he looks like a fully grown man who is genuinely concerned. 'Do you see what I'm saying? I'm telling you *why* the judge adjourned your trial.'

'Don't be absurd.'

'I'll do my best but it won't be easy,' says Rosentreter, reverting to a boyish grin.

'You could start by acting like a proper lawyer. How are you going to handle my defence?'

'First we're going to contest the fine.'

'What's the point? Twenty days' salary is affordable; if we contest it, you'll charge me the same amount in fees. I'd rather pay the fine. I committed the infraction: I'll accept the penalty and put it behind me.'

'I commend your intentions, but that's not the way it works. Law is a game, and everyone plays a part. I'm your defence counsel and as such I intend to defend you.'

'What or whom are you defending me against, Herr Rosentreter?'

'Against the charges laid by the prosecution – and

against the court's intention to hold you responsible for a situation that isn't your fault.'

'I'd rather conduct my own defence.'

'How exactly, if you don't mind me asking?'

'By doing nothing and keeping quiet.'

'That would be madness. You don't seem to grasp what you're up against. They'll accuse you of subverting the Method.'

Shaking her head, Mia raises an index finger and points it at Rosentreter's chin. 'How old are you? Sixteen? We *are* the Method: you, me, everyone. The Method is reason; the Method is good sense. I told the judge, and I'll say it again for your benefit: I'm not against the Method. And for the last time, I'd like be left alone. It's all I'm asking. I'll work things out on my own.'

'Can you do it by tomorrow morning?'

'Maybe not entirely.'

'In that case, you'll need my help.'

'Are you short of clients?'

'On the contrary.'

'Why waste your time on me?'

'I want to help. I take my job seriously. The particulars of your situation fall easily within the criteria for an exemption – a first-year law student could tell you that. Now let's get one thing straight.' He leans forward and pats the air above Mia's shoulder. 'You're not in the least bit to blame. Not even for smoking the stupid cigarette. I'm not going to stand by while they take shots at you.'

Because Rosentreter is so damn right, or because Mia damn well hopes he's right, she finds herself close to tears.

'Thank you,' she says, clearing her throat. 'Taking shots is exactly how I'd describe it. It's good to know we agree on something . . . But I don't want any trouble; I need some time to reflect, that's all.'

'Absolutely, absolutely,' says Rosentreter, beaming. 'You do the thinking; I'll do the dirty work.' When Mia doesn't laugh, he says, 'I was joking. I'll need another signature. Here and here. That's right, Frau Holl.'

Monitored

'Mia!' calls Driss.

'Frau Holl,' says Pollie, 'we were hoping—'

'At least have the decency to stop,' barks Lizzie furiously.

Mia is in a hurry to get to her apartment. With a shopping bag in each hand, she breaks through the blockade of mops and buckets and is about to climb the stairs when Lizzie grabs her sleeve.

'You can't just run away from us!'

'Mia,' says Driss, 'I'm really sorry. I didn't do it on purpose. I really thought your apartment was on fire.'

'I hope you don't think any of us would *denounce* you,' chimes in Pollie.

'Frau Holl,' says Lizzie, 'we're here to help. If there's anything we can do . . .'

Mia makes a break for freedom by stepping to the side. 'Thank you. You're very kind, but there's really no need.'

'Oh, but there is,' says Pollie.

'Of course there is, Frau Holl,' says Lizzie, gripping Mia's sleeve. 'This is a monitored house and we look after each other. Especially if someone happens to be in trouble.'

'Mia,' says Driss, 'you don't understand: it's not the way it seems!'

Driss would like to carry Mia's shopping for her, make her a cup of hot water and explain things from the start. She would like to explain that she, Driss, is Mia's and Kramer's greatest admirer; that she was only trying to save Mia from the flames. Her eyes are glassy with despair.

'It seems pretty straightforward to me,' says Mia to Driss. To the others, she says, 'Thank you, ladies, but you're blocking the stairs.'

'The stairs belong to us as well, you know.'

'This is a monitored house, Frau Holl.'

'It needs to stay that way.'

'Have we made ourselves clear?'

Lizzie tightens her grip as Mia struggles to break free. Mia hugs her shopping bags and rams her shoulder into Lizzie. The movement is too vigorous. Lizzie has a foot on one step and the other a step higher, with buckets everywhere. She falls, buckets clatter and miniature cascades of soapy water drench the landing, while Mia flees up the stairs.

No one calls after her.

You'll pay for that, you'll pay, says an echo in Mia's head.

Centre of Operations

Mia has never had much regard, let alone affection, for her body. The body is a machine, a walking, talking, ingesting apparatus; its principal responsibility is to function without a hitch. Mia herself is at the centre of operations; she looks out through eye-windows and listens through openings in her ears. Every minute of every day she issues instructions in the full expectation that her body will carry them out. One such instruction is to exercise.

Over the past few weeks, her stationary bike has accumulated a backlog of six hundred kilometres. Mia starts pedalling and thinks about — what? For the sake of simplicity, let us assume her thoughts turn to Moritz. The probability that we are right in our assumptions is very high. Mia herself is aware that she has never thought about Moritz so much as now, after his death. She wonders if this is normal. Or whether thinking about her dead brother is a frantic attempt to keep him alive with the power of her mind. Perhaps, though, she isn't trying to save Moritz, but the rest of the world, the future of which depends, as Mia has come to see it, on Moritz continuing to breathe, talk and laugh.

This much Mia has grasped: the centre of command can issue instructions to the body, but not to itself. The head can't stop itself thinking. Mia, in spite of this knowledge, thinks she has a chance. If an overgrown child like Rosentreter can muddle through life, it should surely be possible for someone like her. She cycles faster. The twentieth virtual kilometre is already behind her. She must teach herself to think of Moritz at the *same time* as going about her normal life, not *instead*.

'Seven units of protein,' says the ideal inamorata, who is lying on the couch. She rummages through Mia's shopping bags. 'Ten units of carbohydrate. Three of fruit and veg. Exemplary. We're on the road to recovery, are we?'

'When I'm done with this,' puffs Mia, 'I'll clean and tidy the apartment. You'll see. In a few days, I'll be back to work as normal.'

'Good intentions are peculiar things,' says the ideal inamorata. 'A powerful expression of their own irrelevance.'

'I'd appreciate a little more optimism. "Law is a game, and everyone plays a part." It sounds like Moritz, wouldn't you say?'

'Moritz wanted to be in charge of his own game.'

'You might be right.' Mia wipes the sweat from her forehead with her sleeve. 'In any case, he'll have to resign himself to having his lines rescripted by the rest of us. He's the one who decided not to play.'

'I'd like to propose a different metaphor,' says the ideal inamorata, picking up a protein tube and pretending to quote from the packaging. 'A single cognitive error contains the recommended daily amount of self-delusion for a typical healthy adult.' She lifts her head and looks at Mia. 'Want to know the truth? *This isn't a game.*'

'What do you mean?'

'Come on, Mia, you're not going to fill the yawning crack inside you with Rosentreter and some exercise. The damage runs deeper, Mia. It isn't about you personally; it runs through this country, and it started with the decision that individual pathologies are a luxury we can't afford. You're being eaten away on the inside by the rot at the heart of the system.'

'You represent Moritz, and I respect that,' says Mia. 'You want to keep alive his memory; that's your job. But don't presume to know what I'm like on the inside. Even Moritz didn't understand me. He thought I was weak and conformist.'

'And the truth is . . . ?'

'I'm smart enough to know that fighting the system is narcissistic.'

'The human condition is a pitch-black room in which you crawl around like newborn babies under constant supervision in case you bump heads. Is that what you mean?'

'Pretty much. Where did you get that? It sounds familiar.'

'From your new friend, Heinrich Kramer.'

'Maybe we were wrong about him,' says Mia. 'He's a media personality; he might be entirely different underneath.'

'Appearance versus reality? Not that old chestnut! The person who *appears* to be Kramer, the person responsible for condemning an innocent man, is only a cover for the *real* Kramer, who doesn't agree with any of Kramer's views! Or do you think it was all an unfortunate mistake?'

'What's your problem?' Mia, who has been pedalling furiously, comes to a sudden stop. 'I don't want to argue.'

'What they did to Moritz was either right, or it was wrong,' the ideal inamorata says sharply. 'There's no middle ground. It's up to you to make a decision. Now come on, Mia, darling. Come over here.'

'But I haven't finished.'

'I said *come here*!'

Mia wavers for a moment, then slides from her exercise bike and walks to the couch. The ideal inamorata knocks the shopping to the floor with a sweep of her arm and flicks on the TV.

People's Right to Illness

'We should take a moment to consider what it stands for: PRI or People's Right to Illness, that is, a radical affront to healthy thought.'

The presenter, Wörmer, is half Kramer's age and half as famous. We can tell this from looking at him. Next to Kramer, he looks like the nervous young editor of a school magazine. He has dedicated his career to following in the footsteps of tonight's guest. Wörmer is the host of his own talk show, *What We All Think*. He asked Kramer to appear as his guest, and Kramer agreed. This is the crowning moment of Wörmer's life so far.

'You're an expert on anti-Method activities,' says Wörmer. 'How does it feel to be up against people who are obviously intellectually impaired? Do you worry for your sanity?

'Absolutely not,' says Kramer, his left arm dangling casually over the side of his chair. His right hand holds a glass, which he twists from side to side, sometimes looking into the water as if it were a crystal ball. 'The members of the PRI are in no sense intellectually impaired. We're not talking about outsiders, dropouts or the underprivileged. They're normal people and by no means unintelligent. The PRI isn't a form of organised crime; it's a network. The opponents of the Method work together in loose association. Structurally, it adds to the threat – a movement governed by coincidence and chaos is very difficult to combat.'

'Fascinating,' says Wörmer. 'It makes you wonder how a well-balanced system could give rise to such irrationalism – a twentieth-century throwback, I suppose . . . Well, what else can you tell us about these people, Herr Kramer?'

'You're not far off with your reference to the twentieth century.' Kramer takes a sip of water and nods at a pretty production assistant, who rushes over to refill his glass.

'Turn it off,' says Mia. 'It's the same old PRI hysteria.'

'We're not interested in hysteria,' says the ideal inamorata. 'We're interested in your new friend.'

'The opponents of the Method,' Mia's friend is saying, 'are characterised by a reactionary belief in individual freedom dating back to the twentieth century. The PRI's ideas are grounded in a flawed interpretation of the Enlightenment.'

'But isn't the Method the logical successor to the Enlightenment?'

'Hence the complexity of the situation. Incredible as it sounds, the PRI includes many former adherents of the Method.'

'People in the midst of our society?'

'Precisely.' Kramer looks straight into the camera and his gaze seems to settle on Mia's face. 'People like you and me. Freedom isn't freedom from responsibility, they understand that, but their mistake is to believe that a cancer patient watching himself die by degrees is somehow *free*. We're talking about a person incapable of leaving his bed.'

'Isn't that incredibly cynical?' asks Wörmer, holding up his hands in horror.

'You have to be a cynic to oppose the Method. But there's an important point I'd like to make here: these people aren't malicious; they're ignorant. The unassailable right to health enshrined by the Method is one of humanity's greatest achievements. For example, a woman born thirty-four years ago would have no recollection of physical pain. How can she possibly imagine the grim reality behind the death statistics for 2012? Illness, as far as she is concerned, is a historical phenomenon.'

'*I* was born thirty-four years ago,' remarks Mia.

'Really?' says the ideal inamorata in mock surprise.

'I see what you're saying,' says the presenter. He starts to nod and shows no sign of stopping. 'The very success of the Method, its absolute efficacy, leads people to lose sight of its purpose.'

'Let us suppose for a moment that our thirty-four-year-old woman finds herself in a difficult emotional situation. Her personal needs no longer seem compatible with the demands of the Method. Now, each of us is selfish at heart, and it is only to be expected that in certain situations our personal wishes will be at odds with the common will. However, an intelligent person, precisely *because* of her intelligence, will be reluctant to admit the truth, namely, that her dilemma is an entirely banal and unexceptional conflict of interests, the solution to which is equally banal and unexceptional, consisting, as it invariably does, in admitting an error of logic. Such a person will be inclined to elevate her personal dilemma to a question of fundamental principles; rather than finding fault with herself, she finds fault with the system.'

'That's what I always said to Moritz,' says Mia weakly.

'Another reason for not turning it off,' says the ideal inamorata, clutching the remote control with both hands. 'Mia, you need to ask yourself: which side you are on?'

'What do you want to hear? We both know Kramer is a rabble-rouser! But he isn't the devil: the devil lies in the detail, in a fiendish detail. Kramer is every bit as right – and every bit as wrong – as his opponents.'

'Shush,' says the ideal inamorata.

'So, coming back to the example of the intelligent young woman who starts to doubt the system,' says Wörmer. 'I suppose it's a slippery slope . . . ?'

'It's a vicious circle,' says Kramer. 'Every real or imagined step taken against the Method engenders a reaction that appears to confirm her doubts. It's a very human situation: in the blink of an eye, you can find yourself outside the norm. The correlation between public and private interest has been the focus of comprehensive studies—'

'Including this one,' says the presenter, waving a book at the camera: *Health as the Principle of State Legitimacy* by Heinrich Kramer, Berlin/Munich/Stuttgart, 25th edition. He puts it down when his guest becomes impatient. The author is entitled to be modest in the light of his success.

'According to the Method,' continues Kramer, 'normality refers to the perfect alignment of public and private good.

A person who rejects this definition of normal will be seen by society to fall outside the norm. Life outside the norm is lonely, as you might imagine. Soon after converting to the cause of anti-normalism, our sample woman will feel the need to forge alliances. Her new companions will be drawn from the enemies of the Method.'

'Only a truly great mind can break down complex issues into good hard facts,' says Wörmer, his admiration for Kramer practically lifting him out of his seat. 'One last question, if I may. With the chronological gap to the pre-Method era widening, should we reckon with an upsurge in anti-Method agitation?'

'Undoubtedly; but we're expecting it, and we're prepared. Any intelligent person will understand the scale of the threat. It's important to remind ourselves of the historical conditions that gave rise to the Method.' Kramer jerks a thumb towards the past, which he seems to think lies somewhere behind his chair. He nods his head solemnly as he prepares to confront us with some uncomfortable truths.

'The second Enlightenment came about in the wake of twentieth-century violence and led to the almost total de-ideologisation of society. Notions such as nationhood, religion and family lost their meaning. The era of dismantling had begun. Later, those caught up in the process were surprised to find that the prevailing sentiment at the turn of the millennium was far from triumphant; people felt *less*, not more civilised: isolated and direction-less, closer to the state of nature. Soon everyone was discussing the decline in moral values. Society had lost confidence in itself, and people reverted to fearing each other. Fear was at the heart of people's lives and the core of state politics. The period of dismantling was over, but no one had prepared for rebuilding. The consequences were dire: plummeting birth rates, an increase in stress-related illness, outbreaks of violence and terrorism. Not to mention the privileging of personal interest, the erosion of loyalty and the eventual collapse of the entire social edifice. Chaos, illness and general uncertainty.'

A dark memory flits across Kramer's face, although he knows the story only from his parents.

'The Method got to grips with the problem and provided a solution. It therefore follows that opposing the Method is a retrograde step. These people are reaction-aries, intent on returning society to a state of chaos. They're not waging a campaign against an idea; they're attacking the well-being and safety of every single member of our society. Every attack on the Method is an act of war, and the supporters of the Method are prepared to fight back.'

While the studio audience bursts into enthusiastic applause, the presenter and his guest leave their seats and Mia finally seizes the remote control and hits the off button.

'Well,' says the ideal inamorata. 'Do you see what's going on now?'

Mia looks at her questioningly.

'Your new friend meant *you*.'

The End of the Fish

They often argued, but that day – the day, as Mia later realised, when things started to go wrong – they had a full-blown fight. Every week they would set out for a walk, and every week they would stop at the edge of the exclusion zone and go through their usual ritual. Moritz would stop in front of the sign at the end of the path, stretch out his arms and read the printed warning:

> You are leaving the Controlled Area. This Area has been sterilised in accordance with Article 17 on Public Cleanliness. Anyone who passes beyond this point will be in breach of Article 18 on Infection Containment and will be penalised accordingly.

Then he would add, 'Failure to leave the Controlled Area is evidence of wilful stupidity: your body will be turned to stone and your mind to mush. What are you waiting for, Mia Holl?'

Mia would run away, and he would catch her, still struggling energetically, and lift her off the ground. Carrying Mia, he would charge into the woods, hurtling towards what he called freedom and what was otherwise known as a hygiene risk.

Moritz saw his exercise obligations as a drag. He liked to exercise, but he didn't want his ID chip in his arm communicating with the sensors on the road. Moritz wanted to walk in the woods without accumulating credits. He wanted to go fishing, light a fire and eat his catch. He preferred the taste of his scaly, slightly burnt and amateurishly filleted fish to any protein tube in the supermarket. When they went to the river, Mia would gather some nettles and offer them to her brother as a salad. She would watch as he chomped his way through his unappetising snack. And she would think, though she never said so, that Moritz, although quite probably a little unhinged, was someone you couldn't resist.

That day too Moritz dangled his improvised fishing line into the water, chewed ostentatiously on a blade of grass, and allowed the river, a torrent of possible infections, to wash around his feet. It was warm outside, and Mia found herself leaning back on her elbows and gazing at the sky. Despite the elevated risk of skin cancer, she angled her face towards the sun. The cathedral was decked out with light, and Mia tried not to listen as Moritz filled her in on his blind date with Kristine and her proficiency at what he referred to as 'doggy-style'. When he finally finished, she launched into a short lecture on the purpose and merits of the Central Partnership Agency. She called her brother a reckless pleasure-seeker, an egotist who was fundamentally incapable of loving a woman.

Was her tone a little harsh? Did she go beyond the usual teasing? Sometimes Mia would feel a stab of jealousy when Moritz talked about his dates. On such occasions her tone would be harsher than she intended, though not sufficiently harsh to justify Moritz reacting as he did. The woods were chirping happily and life was good, as good as it always was when the two of them were together. But Moritz was incensed.

'You make me sick,' he said angrily. 'You of all people, accusing me of being incapable of love! The fact is, I'm human and you're not.'

He spoke more urgently, more intensely than usual. He had fire in his eyes and he intoned his words with the passion of a poet.

'Unlike an animal, I can rise above the compulsions of nature. I can have sex without wanting to reproduce. I can decide to take substances that unchain me from my body and allow me, temporarily, to be free. I can disregard my survival instincts and place myself in danger, for nothing more than the challenge and the thrill. To be human, it isn't enough to *exist*, if to exist means simply being here in this world. Man must *experience* his existence. Through pain. Through intoxication. Through failure. By soaring as high as you can. By apprehending the full extent of your power over your own existence – over life, over death. That, my poor, withered sister, is love.'

They'd had this debate more often than they could remember, but never like this. This time the truth was out there on the surface, leaving the core of things empty. Or, to put it another way, it was a matter of packaging. Moritz had stepped outside the carefully balanced game of derision they'd been perfecting since childhood. He'd hurt Mia's feelings, and she didn't intend to back down.

'My poor misguided brother . . . Don't you realise what a hypocrite you are? Apprehending the full extent of your power . . . It won't mean a thing when your heart goes on strike! It's all very well to talk about freedom when you're enjoying the benefits of a risk-free society. While you're making combative speeches, the rest of us are picking up the tab. You're not free; you're hypocritical and gutless!'

'A risk-free society!' Moritz laughed. 'Tell me you didn't say that! Even *you* should know better than to parrot the slogans of those conformists. Life won't be risk-free until we're suspended in liquid growth medium and forbidden from touching each other. What's the point of being safe if we vegetate for the rest of our lives to satisfy someone's warped idea of the norm? If we have just one idea that isn't about our safety, if our minds rise above our physical needs and contemplate something bigger than ourselves, then at least we're living a life of dignity, which in the higher sense is the *only* normal one. You know the worst part, Mia? You're clever enough to understand what I'm saying.'

'That's where you're wrong.' Mia scratched some pebbles from the ground and hurled them into the water. Even as a child she found it irritating when Moritz claimed to know her better than she knew herself. 'I'm clever enough to know that what you're saying is nonsense. What would you rather we thought about? God? The nation? Equality? Human rights? Or maybe you'd like to propose your own ghoulish ideal scraped from the battle-field of humanity's beliefs!'

'I know what this is about,' said Moritz, jutting out his chin and somehow looking down on his sister, even though they were both seated. 'You want everyone to be safe, not because you love your fellow humans, but because you despise them.'

'Quite possibly,' said Mia. 'But you rhapsodise about freedom and higher meaning because you hate who you are. You cloak yourself in phantasmagorical ideals because you can't stand the sight of yourself. You don't want to admit that you despise yourself, so you despise the system. You hate yourself so much you think dying would be fun.'

'It's got nothing to do with fun or with hate,' said Moritz angrily. 'Yes, I could kill myself. The decision to live counts for nothing without the freedom of choosing to die!'

'You have to turn your back on death if you want to think freely. You have to commit to life.'

'You can't be free unless you stop seeing death as the opposite of life. The end of a fishing line and the opposite of a fishing line are two separate things.'

'The end of the fishing line is the end of the fish,' said Mia lightly.

Moritz didn't laugh, didn't look at her, didn't reach out a conciliatory hand. 'The difference,' he said, 'is you've never confronted your own mortality.'

'Not that again.' Mia frowned. 'What happened to you was dreadful; dreadful but unexceptional – and it certainly wasn't enough to give you transcendental wisdom. You were five years old!'

'I was *six*,' said Moritz. 'I was six and I learned to

accept that humans have only one life and a short one at that.'

'Let's not forget you were saved by the conformists you like to scorn. Without the Method, you wouldn't have found a donor. Can't you be grateful?'

'I'm grateful to nature and not the conformists,' said Moritz. 'I'm grateful for an experience that stopped me being as narrow-minded as you. I've got feelings, real feelings.'

Mia looked at him intently. Finally, she touched his shoulder. 'What's wrong with you? You seem so different. You sound very . . .'

'Serious?'

'By your standards, yes.'

'I'm in training,' said Moritz simply.

'For a new you?'

'For Sibylle.'

'I don't understand.'

'Remember what you said just now?'

Suddenly he looked at her with an expression that made the argument implode, leaving fresh air, the smell of warm earth, and the river with a thousand luminous pennies drifting on its back.

'I'm working on being in love,' said Moritz. 'Other people buy plastic roses, regulation perfume or chocolate-free chocolates but she wouldn't like any of that. I'm going to give her a bouquet of words with the smell of freedom and the sweetness of revolution.'

'Now you're making fun of me.'

'For once I'm not. Tonight I'm going to tell her every-thing that I've just told you, only she won't wrinkle her brow and give me dusty answers: she'll stare at me with her big silky eyes and understand every word. I've known her only three days and the things we've written to each other would get us three years in jail. Who cares, so long as we share a cell! She's the one, Mia. I can feel it.'

'What about deep-throating and doggy-style?'

'Hopefully that as well,' said Moritz, laughing. 'Hey, I've got a bite!'

The rod twitched, he held on with both hands and pulled a fish out of the water, splashing and fighting on the end of the line.

'You'll like her, I know.' Moritz leaned across and pressed a kiss to Mia's forehead. Then he picked up a fallen branch and struck the fish on the head. 'If Sibylle thinks the way she writes, she's wackier than me. You'll have two of us to argue with in future.'

The Gavel

'Frau Holl! Frau Holl! Are you with us? Shall I summon a doctor?'

Sophie's dislike of anachronism extends to the use of her gavel. She strikes it three times against her desk, her rage increasing with every strike. The defendant, sitting to the left of the private counsel, looks up in confusion. She looks at the judge's desk, peers at Barker for the prosecution, who is leaning back in his chair, eyebrows edging towards his temples. Finally she fixes her gaze on her own face, which is sitting majestically on her naked body like a religious painting at the top of a column and staring back at her from the screen. If Sophie has a problem with using her gavel, it is nothing compared to knowing that her character analysis was wrong. Mia's soft mouth indicated a love of harmony, her bright eyes were a sign of mental clarity. And now Mia, the defendant, is staring into space. Yet again she has bitten the hand that feeds her. Sophie's hand. This could be either the sign of a person-ality problem or an indication that she is depressed. Sophie can't decide which is worse. Personality problems are a curse; the courthouse would be empty without them. Depression, however, is a corrosive force. People with depression reap the benefits of society's generosity and goodwill, while making a religion of self-pity. Nothing could be further from their minds than overcoming their affliction. They are missionaries of unhappiness: a contagion. According to the Health Code, psychological illness is every bit as pernicious as its physical counterpart. And harder to prove.

'I'm terribly sorry, Your Honour,' says Mia.

Sophie hears Rosentreter whisper soothingly to his client. She almost feels sorry for him. He is an upright, unassuming man, not in the least equipped to deal with a recalcitrant character like Mia Holl.

'What I have here is an appeal against the sentence I imposed,' says Sophie, waving a sheet of paper in the air. 'Signed by you.'

Mia looks uncertainly at Rosentreter, who pokes her gently in the ribs.

'Yes, Your Honour,' she says.

'The penalty imposed for your infractions was extremely lenient.' Hearing the hysteria in her voice, Sophie clears her throat and makes an effort to be professional. 'It was an olive branch.'

'Practically an acquittal,' chimes in Barker.

'Indeed.' Sophie aims a mocking nod in Barker's direction. 'Frau Holl, the sentence was supposed to get you back on track. Is that clear?'

'I suppose so, Your Honour,' says Mia like a puppet whose jaw is worked by strings.

'Enough!' screeches Sophie, and this time she takes satisfaction in using her gavel. 'I'm rejecting your appeal.

And the penalty will be raised to fifty days' wages. As for your abuse of toxic substances—'

'But . . .' says Mia, who has been listening to the judge's pronouncements with increasing amazement, 'but I *am* back on track. I submitted the missing data on sleep and nutrition to the relevant authorities. You've seen my medical and hygiene tests. The bacteria levels in my apartment are within the prescribed range. I'll make up my exercise deficit within the next few days, and—'

'I'm not falling for this again, Frau Holl. Perhaps you could explain why you're appealing against a sentence that my superiors deemed unconscionably lax?'

'Objection, Your Honour,' says Rosentreter. 'The defendant can't be held responsible for the judge's professional reputation.'

'But—' says Mia.

'Objection upheld. I hereby terminate my examination of Frau Holl at the request of her lawyer. It brings the matter to a mercifully swift conclusion.'

'Kind of you to do my job,' says Barker.

'No one asked you to comment,' says Sophie sharply. Turning back to Rosentreter, she says, 'The next infraction: abuse of toxic substances. Your plea?'

'Guilty,' says Rosentreter.

'But I don't see why . . .' says Mia.

'You smoked a cigarette, didn't you?' says Rosentreter softly. 'You admitted to it last week.'

'Of course,' says Mia, 'but I thought you said—'

'You were adamant you wanted to deal with it yourself – I told you there was only one possible way of avoiding official intervention.' The counsel for the defence looks apologetically at Sophie. 'Frau Holl is appealing against the bringing of the charge. We refer Your Honour to the Health Code, Article 28. We're seeking an exemption.'

'An exemption!' Barker slaps his hand against his desk in amusement. 'Honestly, Rosentreter, couldn't you talk her out of it?'

The colour has vanished from Sophie's ruddy cheeks. Sophie doesn't like herself when she loses her cool. Anger is an unhealthy emotion that runs counter to her natural disposition. Knowing this only adds to her fury.

'The defendant is apparently of the opinion that her actions are beyond the jurisdiction of this court,' she says coldly. 'She also seems to think that the judge is incapable of assessing her personal situation, whereas the judge in question has bent over backwards on her account.'

Mia's mouth is half open. Right now, the arrangement of her features says nothing about her need for harmony; she simply looks out of her depth. She also looks stupid – stupid in an obstinate way. She looks from one to the other like a dog that can't quite remember which of them is her master. At last she gestures towards Rosentreter. 'My lawyer told me . . .'

'My client needs peace and quiet,' says Rosentreter, picking a sheet of paper from his desk. 'She wants time to reflect. She thinks the interference of the authorities will be detrimental to her recovery.'

'Your Honour!' Barker leans across his desk. 'Surely it's time for the defendant's comments to be recorded in her file?'

'Agreed.' Sophie turns on her digital recorder and places

it on the desk. 'Herr Rosentreter, on what grounds is your client seeking exemption?'

As soon as Rosentreter starts speaking, his words flash up on the screen. 'Frau Holl has been placed in an exceptional situation by the system: to wit, her brother was taken from her through the implementation of the Method. She would like to deal with the fallout from the aforementioned incident without the intervention of the Method and its associated institutions, hence the application for exemption in accordance with Article 28.'

'Is this true?' asks Sophie, leaning over her lectern. 'Do you believe your brother died through the implementation of the Method?'

'Causally speaking, yes,' says Mia. 'But it doesn't mean I . . .'

'It doesn't mean you can cut yourself off from the Method and its public institutions – absolutely right, Frau Holl. Your lawyer will have explained that Article 28 was designed to rectify miscarriages of justice and not—'

'Your Honour,' cuts in Barker's whiny voice, 'the judge is under no obligation to remedy the failings of the defence.'

Sophie erupts. 'I've had enough of your fault-finding,' she bellows. 'This isn't a university canteen, where you can show off. Official caution in accordance with Article 12 – otherwise known as contempt of court.'

The gavel comes down hard on the desk. Sophie lays it aside in disgust.

'The defendant's application for exemption is rejected,' she says, barely keeping her composure. 'I won't have my courtroom treated like a circus. The defendant is found guilty of abusing toxic substances and is sentenced to a two-year suspended term. I trust the penalty meets with the prosecution's approval.'

'In every respect,' says Barker through gritted teeth.

'Excellent. Incidentally, I'd like to remind Frau Holl that Method Defence is automatically informed of any attempt to apply for an exemption through recourse to Article 28. The court is now closed.'

Which Side Are You On?

'There was a line from a song in the good old days,' says the ideal inamorata. '*Which side are you on?* You should adopt it as your anthem.'

It is probably somewhere approaching midday, maybe a little later, although at this point the hour is of little interest to those in the room. There is a springtime warmth to the day. The door to the roof garden is open, admitting balmy air. The self-satisfied buzzing of a bee can be heard from the flowerpots. Rosentreter watches from the doorway as the insect flits between the artificial petals, which exude a synthetic aroma known as 'primrose'.

Is Mia's lawyer in the apartment by invitation? Not really: Mia's lawyer is in her apartment because he walked her home. They were on their way out of the courthouse when Mia stopped on the steps and stared at her surroundings, as if seeing the city with new eyes. And while she stared, she talked to herself: she had slowed down, she said, to a tenth of her usual speed, and that was the reason why the days were passing ten times faster, cyclists were going ten times faster, and people were talking at ten times their usual speed, so that she, Mia, could no longer make sense of anything. The brain, she said, was just a muscle, like any other. Rosentreter stepped in before she drew attention to herself by sitting on the stairs. He looked up her address in his file and walked her home.

Right now Mia is forcing down a couple of brightly coloured pills. Her eyes are closed. Modern medicine provides an answer to every existential problem; any remaining uncertainty can be clarified by only one man − Rosentreter. His lanky frame is slightly stooped, as if he were trying to make himself shorter. He runs his hand through his floppy hair for the hundredth time.

'Happy now?' asks Mia.

'I've been admiring the view.' Rosentreter scatters a few loose hairs and turns to face Mia.

'I'm not interested in the view,' she says. 'I want to know if you *like* playing the torturer.'

'Interesting you should mention torture. It may surprise you to learn that the introduction of torture was a milestone in the development of the modern criminal trial.'

'Who does he take me for?' says Mia to the ideal inamorata. 'He's as bad as the rest.'

'I like him better than the other one,' says the ideal inamorata. 'There's something about his eyes − like a small boy in a toyshop.'

'This man,' says Mia loudly, pointing at Rosentreter, 'sabotaged my case.'

'I know the business with torture sounds absurd,' says Rosentreter, raising a hand to his chin as if he were giving a seminar on legal history, 'but it's absolutely true. It followed the abolition of trial by ordeal − *judicium*

Dei. Thereafter man, not God, was supposed to sit in judgement over humankind. But how could ordinary humans without divine knowledge be relied upon to divine the truth? Confession was the only reliable indicator of guilt. Sadly, defendants couldn't be counted upon to confess, so the system came up with a means of . . .' Rosentreter smiles to himself '. . . probing their conscience.'

'If you don't mind,' says Mia, 'I'd like to get back to the workings of *my* case. That's enough of a torture for me.'

'The use of torture was a casualty of humanism,' says Rosentreter, unabashed. 'It left us with a problem, though. We're still not really comfortable with punishing people who protest their innocence to the last.'

'We don't know each other,' says Mia, taking a step towards him. 'I have no idea who you are. Or whose cause you're hoping to serve by putting on this pantomime.'

'I'm the counsel for the defence, and you're the defendant. If we follow the rules of semantics, that makes me the counsel for *your* defence.'

'You promised to get me out of this mess,' says Mia. She jabs her finger at him in a prosecutorial fashion. 'And now, thanks to you, I'm in an even bigger hole. Perhaps you can offer me some advice, Herr Rosentreter. Can I sue you for what you've done?'

'Of course. If you're clever about it, you could have me disbarred for this morning's performance.'

'Marvellous,' says Mia sarcastically. 'In that case, I instruct you to sue yourself.'

'You may wish to consider where your interests lie — and how you intend to defend them.'

'Exactly what I've been saying,' exclaims the ideal inamorata. 'Which side are you on?'

'Your brother was charged with sexually motivated homicide and sentenced to indefinite *vita minima*. Do you think he did it?'

'I'm not prepared to discuss it with you.'

'You think he was innocent, don't you?' Rosentreter closes the patio door. 'You think he was innocent because you knew him. *Him*, in other words: his soul, his heart, his spirit. None of which play any role in human inter-action, according to the Method.'

Mia clutches her head, a battleground between her ragged nerves and the numbing effect of the pills. 'Why does everyone on the planet see me as their political confessor?'

'Because,' the ideal inamorata says simply, 'your time has come.' She flings out her arms dramatically, just as Moritz would have done. 'Warning, you are entering the real world. Small pieces represent a choking hazard.'

'I wish you'd shut up,' snaps Mia.

'Good,' says Rosentreter, satisfied. 'It's OK to get angry. After what happened this morning, we're closer than you think.'

'And what *did* happen exactly?'

'It was a playground scrap.' Rosentreter holds up his hands. 'Small children throwing sand in each other's eyes. It's time to throw down the gauntlet to the professionals. We're taking this further.'

'*We?*' exclaims Mia.

'What are you trying to say?'

'I'm giving up. Or rather: I gave up long ago. Let me

say again: no! I can't give up because there isn't and never has been anything I want to achieve.'

'You *can't* give up; that's precisely the problem, Frau Holl. Don't you understand what they were threatening you with this morning? Method Defence. They want you branded as a security threat.'

'That is entirely your fault.'

'We're not going to let them get away with it!' Rosentreter is waving his hands excitedly. 'What sort of a system kills a man and withholds the right for his sister to grieve on her own?'

'Are you speaking as a lawyer?'

'As a human being, Frau Holl.'

'Grow up, Rosentreter. Looking for the human condition is like knocking at a door when you know no one's home. You wait for a bit, peer inside and call out: Is anyone there? Then you go.'

'The Method killed the human and left a mask in his place,' says the ideal inamorata. 'You're an exception, dear heart. You're human and I love you for it.'

'It's all right for you,' says Mia. 'You do nothing but lounge around all day, safe in the knowledge that you don't have a blood group! No one wants to collect your data or monitor your exercise! You don't even have an immune system.'

'Frau Holl,' Rosentreter says soothingly, 'stop talking to your shoes. Look at *me*, talk to *me*. The Method is committed to serving humanity − Article 1 of the Code. At the next hearing, the court is going to reflect on some matters of principle.'

'Your eyes,' says Mia.

'What about them?' Rosentreter raises a hand to his face.

'They're shining.'

'It's the sunlight.'

'This isn't a defence.' She glares at him. 'This is a crusade.'

'Maybe a crusade is what's necessary.'

'For whom?' she demands.

'For everyone.'

'I'm going to ask you again,' says Mia sharply. 'Who are you? A lunatic? A PRI activist with black robes and a briefcase? Or just a little sadist who thinks it's funny to jump up and down on the wreckage of my life?'

Rosentreter clears his throat. 'I'm unhappy,' he says.

'Get him to explain,' says the ideal inamorata.

'You'd better explain,' says Mia.

'I'd rather not,' says Rosentreter.

'You can turn my life into a combat zone,' says Mia, starting to shout. 'You can cart me to the coliseum on the back of your legal strategies and unleash me on the opposition like an untamed beast. But I've got a right to know why.'

'OK,' says the lawyer, and he sits down next to the ideal inamorata on the couch.

Inadmissible

Mia sits down at her desk and holds her head in her hands, as if her neck were no longer able to take the strain. There is silence for a few moments. Halfway round the world, the Amazon is emptying into the Atlantic at a rate of two hundred million litres per second. You can practically feel it in Mia's living room. Rosentreter is biting his nails, although nail biting is prohibited because of the dangers of infection.

'We don't see each other very often,' he says at last. 'We're in a long-distance relationship, but without the relationship. Distance is all we have. It's like playing battleships inside our heads without a pen or paper.'

'I can't believe I'm hearing this,' says Mia.

'Who would?' says Rosentreter sympathetically. 'After all, individuals with non-complementary immune systems can't fall in love – it's scientifically proven. I'm MHC class 1, B11, which makes me a match for A2, A4 and A6. Then along comes the love of my life, a woman like cold water on burnt skin. Major histocompatibility complex B13. We didn't even apply for an exemption: we wouldn't have stood a chance.'

'I can't believe it,' says Mia again. 'You're up in arms about a trivial MHC discrepancy, is that it?'

'It's not trivial,' says the ideal inamorata.

'Your love is inadmissible!' says Mia, raising her voice. 'Is that the extent of your personal tragedy, the motivation for your crusade?'

'If you want to put it like that: yes.'

'A temporary misalignment of the individual's wishes with the common will,' says the ideal inamorata. 'That's what Kramer would call it.'

'When are you going to wake up?' says Mia, her voice still raised. 'In the olden days, a princess would marry the king and share a bed with the privy counsellor; it's been happening for centuries!'

'You don't understand,' says Rosentreter. 'This isn't about sex; I *love* this woman! I want us to be together; I don't want to hide our relationship. I want children.'

'It's the same old story! The peasant girl and the lord of the manor, the nun and the gardener, brothers and sisters, the schoolgirl and her teacher, the grown man and his best friend: they all *loved* each other. And these days thousands of people love the wrong immune system. Everyone wants to be happy, and sometimes the rules won't allow it. It's the same as it ever was. It's normal, Rosentreter, normal!'

'According to the Method, inadmissible love is a capital offence. If we were to express our love physically, we'd be punished in the same way as people who spread disease.'

'You think you've got a problem? You don't know the first thing about suffering, Rosentreter. You think you can change a situation that's been going on for hundreds of years? *You*, of all people!'

'It's a ridiculous situation!'

'It's more ridiculous to think you can fight it. You're an arrogant fool, Rosentreter. Indulge your illicit passion, but do it discreetly – like everyone else! No one wants to hear about it. The world isn't interested in your personal affairs.'

'Frau Holl, if you don't mind, I'm going to step outside the lawyer–client relationship for a moment. I'm Lutz, by the way.'

Mia looks at him doubtfully. At last she extends a hand. 'Mia,' she says.

'Lutz,' says Rosentreter again.

They shake hands briefly and let go.

'Mia, I've got something to say to you.' Rosentreter raises his voice to a shout. 'You're a bitter, lonely rationalist and you don't know a thing about happiness! I pity you, Mia Holl.'

'Cripes,' says the ideal inamorata.

'Fine,' says Mia furiously. 'I'm a rationalist! Maybe I'm bitter and lonely as well. But if you insist on pitying me, pity me for this!'

She jumps up, grabs a photograph from her desk and drops it into Rosentreter's lap. It is a picture of Moritz on the end of a length of fishing twine. Those unfamiliar with hanging will need to take a second look. A person who hangs himself loses all humanity from his face. His tongue swells to three times its usual size and protrudes from his mouth; his eyes, similarly intent on escaping, leave their sockets. The overall skin colour is blue. Rosentreter looks from the corpse to Mia and back again. In the competition for the greatest personal tragedy, he has lost.

'It's hard to bear,' he says softly.

'Since Moritz died,' says Mia, 'I haven't seen the moon. I look out of the window, and it's gone. Do you think it's abandoned us and journeyed into space? I wouldn't blame it.'

Rosentreter is on his feet as well. He walks slowly towards Mia, as if she were an animal that might bolt at the slightest wrong move.

'Before we all set off for space together,' he says, 'I'd like to look at Moritz's files. I could go over the evidence, maybe reopen the case.'

The ideal inamorata sits bolt upright. 'Could you prove his innocence?'

'Who knows, I might be able to prove his innocence. Listen, Mia, I wouldn't be doing it for you. I've been waiting for years to wrong-foot the Method. All I need . . .'

'If he's really prepared to do it,' says the ideal inamorata, 'we'll do anything, *anything*.'

'A chance is all I need.'

The doorbell rings and Rosentreter stiffens. Mia hurriedly stuffs the photo into a drawer.

Snails

The fear leaves Rosentreter's body, strides once around the room and enforces an unnatural hush. If the defence counsel were to reflect on the matter, he would not be surprised to find himself looking at this particular person, a man who is better informed about Mia's application for exemption than the minister of state. But Rosentreter doesn't have time to reflect, mainly because it takes him too long. Being nice requires a certain slowness, as well as an absence of courage.

'Santé, one and all,' says Kramer.

'Hello,' says Mia.

'Santé,' murmurs Rosentreter.

'Not him again,' says the ideal inamorata.

Kramer looks fantastic. There are two main reasons for this: first, his hat and stick, which are intended to convey the look of a casual *flâneur*; and second, his almost offensively buoyant mood. He is standing taller than usual and his smoothly shaven cheeks are aglow with the sunny confidence of a well-fed baby. He strolls into the apartment with a silent fanfare.

'Well, well,' he says, pointing to Rosentreter as if to call attention to an interesting work of art. 'So the loyal defender of justice is here as well. You're always at hand when there's a private interest to be protected, right, Rosentreter?'

It would be obvious to anyone that Rosentreter is afraid of Kramer. He backs away from him as if he were contagious, only to find himself sitting on the sofa, which has inserted itself obligingly between him and the ground. Rosentreter has known Kramer for years and he knows his gaze, a gaze that distinguishes between the Method's friends and enemies with the uncanny alertness of a sleepwalker finding his path. Loving the wrong woman isn't actually illegal, provided it is done from afar, but it makes a person look suspicious. It is well known that 'love' is merely another word for an immunologically favourable match. Any other type of relationship is diseased. Rosentreter's love is a virus that could contaminate society. Over time, he has realised that true loneliness lies not in the separation from his loved one, but in concealing his impossible longings. Unfortunately, Kramer's ears are almost as sharp as his eyes. In the ensuing silence, Rosentreter tortures himself with the thought that Kramer could have been eavesdropping outside for a while.

Thankfully, Kramer's attention seems to be elsewhere. He turns to Mia.

'Frau Holl,' he says, 'I'm afraid I've got bad news.'

'Break it to me gently,' she says.

Kramer walks towards her. For a moment, it looks as if he is about to infringe Article 44 of the hygiene laws regarding mouth-to-cheek contact, but he adjusts his course and walks straight past her, removing his gloves and placing them with his hat and stick on the desk.

'The profile piece we talked about earlier. I'm afraid it won't happen. Things have moved on.'

Without stopping to ask permission, he strolls into the kitchen to make himself a cup of hot water.

'It's a pleasure to see you anyway,' he calls through the door. 'For an old news hound like me, the commotion you're causing is an absolute treat.'

'He's the one causing the commotion,' says Mia with her eyes on Rosentreter.

'Interesting,' says Kramer, poking his head round the door. His eyebrows soar upwards in two sweeping arcs. The ideal inamorata raises her eyebrows and mimics his astonishment.

'What profile piece?' asks Rosentreter quickly.

'It was his idea to apply for an exemption,' says Mia.

'Anyone else for hot water?' asks Kramer.

'Please,' says Mia.

'Thank you,' says Rosentreter with a shake of the head.

'I hope he's not causing problems,' says Kramer, returning with two steaming cups. 'I can arrange for him to be replaced. I'd love to know what he's been telling you for the past thirty minutes.'

The temperature must be rising in Rosentreter's part of the room. He runs a finger around his collar and at the same time tries to maintain a professional air. Kramer is leaning against the desk and looking expectantly at Mia over the rim of his cup. Mia is looking at her lawyer, whose face is in a state of hopeless disarray. For a moment, the idea of getting rid of Rosentreter holds a certain appeal.

'Mia!' says the ideal inamorata in a warning tone.

Startled, Mia shakes her head as though surprised at herself. 'Rosentreter's told me nothing,' she says at last. 'We were discussing the evidential weight of a defendant's confession.'

'In other words,' says Kramer, 'you were discussing your brother's case. Well, at least he wasn't *tortured*, which is a mercy, don't you think?' Before Mia can reply, he chuckles and carries on. 'These days we can be thankful that new forms of evidence have replaced the confession. I'm talking about modern-day data collection, of course. It's impossible to gather too much information.' He pauses. 'Come on, Rosentreter, surely you disagree? No . . . ? You astonish me. Usually I have to waste my time explaining that data collection is essential for protecting individuals from false allegations. The more detailed the information about a person, the more fairly we can judge. Isn't that right, Frau Holl?'

'I think so,' says Mia.

'Good.' Kramer sets his cup on the table. 'Why don't you tell me about your brother?'

The ideal inamorata catches her breath and practically chokes. Meanwhile, Rosentreter gets up from the sofa and adjusts his suit. 'My client doesn't intend to discuss—'

Mia looks steadily at Kramer. 'Why would I talk to you about Moritz?'

'Because you realise the value of more detailed information,' says Kramer amicably, showing his teeth as he smiles. 'And because you wouldn't want me to leap to any conclusions about why a person would turn down a perfectly simple request.'

Rosentreter is standing right in front of Kramer and trying to look more imposing than he is. 'You have no right to interrogate my client in her apartment,' he says in an unnaturally deep voice.

'What's the big deal, Rosentreter?' Kramer, still in excellent spirits, leaves the desk and starts to pace around the room. 'I thought you were interested in Moritz Holl?'

'I'm interested in my client.'

'Really?' Kramer walks around the exercise bike and checks the backlog on the display. 'Yesterday you asked to see the prosecution's files on Moritz Holl.'

'It was essential for my client's defence.'

'You weren't digging up dirt for the second round?'

'You're the expert on dirt, not me.'

'In a sense, yes,' says Kramer, unruffled. He continues his perambulation, pausing to examine the books on the shelf.

'Gentlemen.' Mia's head has been flicking back and forth as if she were watching a tennis match. 'What is this about?'

'It's about *more*,' says Kramer. 'It's about the significance of Moritz Holl's trial. Isn't that right, Rosentreter? You're in it for the glory.' He swivels round suddenly and fixes the lawyer's face with eyes as clear as glass. 'Well, deny it, if you will!'

Rosentreter bows his head, whereupon Kramer nods and returns to the desk.

'Frau Holl,' he says genially, 'truth is subjective, even in a court of law. *Knowing* and *believing* are remarkably similar – if not, in fact, the same. In difficult cases, therefore, clever people will judge the truth according to its usefulness, not validity.'

'What are you saying?' asks Mia.

'Your brother,' says Kramer, 'is still in our thoughts, albeit for different reasons. He was so damned convincing.'

'He'll be proposing a self-help group in a moment,' says the ideal inamorata.

'In the case of Moritz Holl,' says Kramer, 'your lawyer is gathering evidence against the Method and I'm working in its defence. Opposing forces often converge – for example, right here in this apartment.'

'You mean, at my brother's grave.'

'Why not? Yes, we've come together in this apartment to look for the truth at Moritz's grave. But perhaps you can help us, Frau Holl. What was he *really* like?'

'He loved nature,' says Mia.

'Don't you dare discuss Moritz with that monster!' exclaims the ideal inamorata.

Mia turns to face her. 'Isn't it my role in the world to talk about Moritz?'

'Not to *him*,' says the ideal inamorata. 'He thinks Moritz posed a danger to society; he's fishing for proof.'

'Then we'll prove the opposite,' says Mia. 'Humans are essentially the packaging for memories; I'm the packaging for Moritz.'

The ideal inamorata doesn't reply.

Rosentreter clears his throat uncomfortably and opens his mouth to speak, but Kramer stops him with a warning glance that Mia doesn't see. For a moment, the two adversaries exchange understanding looks.

Mia gets up quickly and walks to the window. 'Moritz

loved nature. As a child, he spent hours studying a single leaf or a beetle. Do you know how many different sorts of beetle you can find in one bush?'

'Loving nature is a necessary precursor to loving humanity,' Kramer prompts.

'Moritz loved all living things. When he was little he kept snails in a wooden box and gave them names. He said their slowness made them strong. They used to escape from the box at night-time by lifting the lid with their shells.'

'Snails take their houses wherever they go,' says the ideal inamorata dreamily. 'Moritz would have liked that.'

'While he was sleeping they slithered around the room. Sometimes he woke in the morning with a snail on his cheek; it made him smile. I thought it was disgusting. We shared a room.'

'There's nothing disgusting about loving living creatures.' Kramer has been sifting through the papers on Mia's desk. Carefully, he opens a drawer. 'Gastropods aren't known for their warlike tendencies or weapons of mass destruction, which is more than can be said for man.'

'Moritz took more or less the same view. He thought nobody understood him – our parents, his friends, me. When he was little, he talked more to plants and animals than to us.'

'But you were his favourite animal,' says the ideal inamorata. 'He named most of the garden after you. Trees, bushes, flowers, birds, worms – they were all called Mia.'

Mia nods and presses the balls of her hands into her

eyes. 'When he got sick, the snails had to go. We had doctors in the house, and my parents were worried about the consequences. Moritz never forgave them.'

'Sick?' queries Rosentreter, surprised. 'It isn't mentioned in the files.'

Kramer shrugs, signalling that Moritz's illness is news to him as well.

'He was cured,' says Mia. 'There was no hereditary component. My parents had the incident deleted from his files.'

'Damned researchers,' says Kramer. 'They should have picked up on it. If I'd known he was sick—'

'He got better,' objects Mia.

'Once sick, always sick,' says Kramer. 'It sticks with you.'

'What stuck with me,' says Mia, 'is that the Method saved his life.'

'His life? What was wrong with him?' asks Rosentreter.

'Leukaemia,' says Mia, turning away from the window. Her gaze falls on Kramer, who is busy examining the photograph of Moritz with his head in a noose.

'The show is officially over,' she says. 'Sorry to interrupt your snooping, but I hope you found it helpful.'

'Very.' Kramer brushes a few specks of dust from his sleeve.

Rosentreter places a finger on his chin and stares ahead, deep in thought. The ideal inamorata looks at his profile and seems to be thinking as well. Leu-kae-mi-a. The climate of the room has been transformed by the rare conjunction of syllables. But Kramer, clever Kramer, is oblivious to the change. He has collected his hat and stick and is busy pursuing new goals.

'You spoke with the eloquence of a poet. You don't mind if I quote you?' he says, his fingers already on the handle.

With that, he is gone.

Ambivalence

Mia's attitude towards Kramer is *ambivalent*, to use a word beloved of the undecided. She cannot even say that she dislikes him. In fact, earlier that day, when he bent over her attentively to hand her a cup of freshly brewed water, a ritual that assumed an almost absurd perfection in his hands, it seemed to her briefly that she could love him. Not because of his manners — good manners being an agreeable way of disguising whatever one happens to be thinking at the time. And not because of his looks, which like all things of beauty were eroded by familiarity, so that after meeting him for the first time, Mia was unable to find him attractive or unattractive but simply and undeniably *there*. No, Mia was impressed by the way in which he could serve a cup of water as if it were a sacred act. The attention he lavished on a seemingly unimportant action spoke of a wholehearted and uncon- ditional engagement with the world which Mia, if she is honest, admires. Kramer puts himself wholly and unconditionally into everything he does — walking, talking, standing, dressing. He thinks and speaks with a ruthlessness that makes no attempt to find dialectical excuses for the eternal uncertainty of humankind. Anyone who claims that truth is dependent on usefulness, anyone who openly admits that knowing and believing are essentially the same for limited beings such as humans, is clearly a nihilist in a class of his own.

Mia replicates his perambulation of her apartment and tries to see her belongings, books and papers through the eyes of a reporter. She too is a nihilist, but in her case, the absence of objective truth leads not, as with Kramer, to an outlook of unconditionality, but to an agonising feeling that nothing is fixed. Mia can find reasons for everything as well as its opposite. She can justify or criticise any given concept or thought; she can argue for and against both sides; in fact, Mia could play chess with or without an opponent and never run out of moves. For a long time now she has believed that a person's character consists mainly of rhetoric, but, unlike Kramer, she has never been tempted to apply her conclusions in any particular way. Deep down she suspects that she and Kramer are cut from the same cloth: that she reached a certain point and stopped, whereas Kramer simply carried on. As if he thought there was a goal, as if he thought there was something worth wanting. The crucial question as to what Kramer wants, as to *what anyone might want*, seems to Mia to find its mystical answer in the perfect way of serving a cup of hot water. For the duration of a few seconds, she was enormously attracted to Kramer.

Either side of those few seconds, which is how we get to the ambivalence, Mia felt a mild revulsion. It would be possible to rewrite, or in Mia's case, mentally reshuffle, the information above. The same starting point could be used to construct a different set of arguments; the black chess pieces could be swapped for the white. Then Kramer, the icon of unconditionality, would be an empty striving with a void at its heart. A snoop. A pathetic creature.

While Mia continues to pace around the room, the ideal inamorata raises herself on her elbows and remonstrates with her. '*An answer contained in the perfect way of serving hot water? Attracted to your brother's killer?* Do you call yourself a woman?'

'Rousseau,' says Mia from the bookcase. 'With a dedication from Moritz at the front. Dostoevsky, Orwell, Musil. Kramer. Agamben, also from Moritz. I haven't read it.'

'You're not a woman,' says the ideal inamorata. 'A woman knows she's a woman without checking between her legs.'

'Only 120 kilometres to go,' says Mia from the stationary bike. 'The backlog will be cleared in a couple of days.'

'Did they take out your brain so your thoughts could go round in circles? *Cut from the same cloth* . . . He's your enemy, Mia! Call yourself human?'

'Fine,' says Mia from her desk. 'I'm not human and I'm not a woman.' She examines the papers that Kramer inspected earlier. 'But I'm not a terrorist either.' She picks up Moritz's picture and holds it to the light. Behind her, the ideal inamorata blends into the dusk; she keeps perfectly still, as if she weren't there.

'I'm just the one who was left behind,' says Mia softly, while outside the sky darkens with memory.

Without the Tears

Mia was still at her desk when the doorbell rang. Startled, she looked at her watch: a few minutes after midnight. This was no ordinary ringing: more the sound of a breakdown. *Shriek, shriek*, it screeched, at regular intervals, relentlessly, as if it would never end. Mia hurried to the door. Moritz was on the landing. He was watching his index finger on the doorbell, as it rang and rang. Mia grabbed his hand. Silence at last. We have a few seconds to work out who is standing at the door. The Murder Night, waiting to be let in. Past tense, of course.

'What's the matter with you? Don't just stand there, Moritz!'

Moritz didn't answer. He took a single step towards her, only to stop in the doorway and stare. He seemed to be seeing the apartment for the first or last time. We can confirm it was the last. Mia took him by the arm and steered him to the sofa.

'Well? Tell me about it. Tell me about *her*. What was her name again?'

'Sibylle.'

'Did you like her? Was she nice?'

'She was dead.'

Mia and Moritz looked at each other. For a few moments, it seemed as if the last scrap of meaning had been emptied out of language, as if what Moritz had said to his sister had no possible meaning in her mind. Time passed, the Earth turned a little further on its axis, a few more people died across the globe, and a few more were born. Then Mia gave Moritz a little shove, and he crumpled.

'What – what do you mean?' she asked.

'Crazy, isn't it?' he said. 'If she were alive, there'd be a million things I'd want to tell you, but now . . . well, there's practically nothing left to say.'

'Pull yourself together and tell me what happened!'

'Fine,' he said wretchedly, 'I'll tell you what happened – but don't expect me to cry. I couldn't cry. Not even at the police station. Promise you'll believe me, even without the tears?'

'Of course,' Mia assures him.

'The girl with the silky eyes. You remember? The one I wanted to go to jail with; freedom paired. She's still here.' He clutched his head. 'She's *in* here. There isn't much else to say.'

He fell silent again. Mia was so upset she had to swallow three times. This was the worst possible time to prove to Moritz that she wasn't the cold-hearted rationalist he thought. No, Mia would have to be strong – to weather anything, like a rock in the storm.

'You'd arranged a place to meet . . .' she said.

'Beneath the South Bridge. That's where I met them all. When a train goes by you can feel the earth shake and you can cling to each other. I was excited and took a detour so as not to arrive too early. At first I assumed she was late or she'd left. But she was lying on the ground. She was naked from the waist down. I took her by the shoulders, lifted her up and laid her back on the ground. She was warm and soft. After a while, I thought to feel her wrists, her neck. I'd forgotten that humans are supposed to have a pulse.'

'Oh, Moritz.'

'The police showed up much later. I had plenty of time to sit beside her and wait. We got on well. She was pretty, prettier than her photo.'

Moritz rubbed his eyes, his cheeks, his scalp as if he were terribly tired, barely able to speak. When he was done, he looked at Mia.

'I was sitting beside a dead body, and I felt close to her, closer than I'd ever felt to anyone. We had so much in common, more than just love. We shared her death.'

He held out his hand and Mia took it.

'Do you think I'm crazy?'

'The world is crazy,' said Mia, 'not you.'

For a while they listened to the emptiness filling the room. Then Mia took a deep breath.

'You were at the police station ... What did they want?'

Moritz started to answer; then he paused, a wave of astonishment rippling over his face. He pulled away his hand.

'Why?'

'It's important.'

'What, in *your* opinion, would the police want with me?'

'Don't be silly, this isn't about what *I* think.'

'Mia Holl, were you even listening to me?'

'Why were you there?'

'I found the body, Mia. Don't you get it? I'm a witness. The police wanted a witness statement. Seems logical, or isn't it logical enough for you?'

'Moritz!'

'You're my sister. You said you'd believe me.'

They got up quickly. Mia ran after him as he hurried to the door. His back was a glyph of anger and despair.

'I'm sorry,' called Mia. 'I'm just worried about you. You know what I'm like. Always worrying. You know you can always talk to me! You can sleep here if you like!'

But Moritz was gone.

'This is your home as well, Moritz,' said Mia to the closed door. 'I'm your home.'

Our Home

Mia still has her ear to the door and is whispering something about Moritz and it being his home and how it was all a mistake, when the doorbell rings again: shriek, shriek. When Mia throws open the door, it isn't night any more, it's broad daylight, and Moritz isn't standing in front of her; it's the Present, this time in triplicate. All three are wearing hygiene masks; two retreat onto the landing to create more distance between themselves and Frau Holl.

'Mia,' says the one who hasn't moved, 'I didn't want to come.'

'Driss,' says Pollie, 'we agreed to stick together.'

'No, we didn't,' says Driss. To Mia she says, 'They forced me.'

'Let me do the talking,' says Lizzie. 'Good morning, Frau Holl.'

'Good morning,' says Mia. Her voice is immeasurably weary. She can guess what the neighbourly deputation is going to ask her. She would have slammed the door already if it weren't for Driss's eyes: two round mirrors of devotion, gazing out above her mask. Driss's eyes are an addiction. Besides, Mia would like to know exactly which part of the story has prompted her neighbours to make their visit now.

'It's a great photo,' says Driss. 'You look lovely! You made the front page!' She reaches for the newspaper, but Pollie whisks it away.

'There's a photo of me in *The Healthy Mind?*' Mia extends a hand, causing Lizzie and Pollie to take another step backwards.

'More importantly,' says Lizze, '*this* arrived today.' She pulls a letter from her tabard and holds it up with both hands. From the look on her face, it could easily be a message from the Almighty, except God, of course, is dead. 'Date, dear Frau so-and-so, with regard to, and so forth. Listen to this: "It has come to our attention that a resident of your block has been convicted for breaching the Health Code. Infractions of this nature may prejudice your status as a monitored household and will be taken into consideration when you apply to renew your licence next year."'

'Who cares about the letter?' says Driss. 'The article is great. It was written by your friend. Do you think he'll call again soon?'

'*I* care about the letter,' says Pollie from behind Lizzie. 'You're not the only one who lives here, Frau Holl.'

'It's *our* house,' says Lizzie. 'We put a lot of effort into keeping it nice.'

'Looking after it, cleaning it.'

'It's nothing personal. It's just important to be considerate.'

'Let me see the article,' says Mia.

'Relocation would be in everyone's best interests,' says Lizzie. 'Including yours.'

'I beg your pardon,' says Mia. Behind her, in the living room, the ideal inamorata laughs.

'I think you should stay,' says Driss. 'Not everyone is the sister of a celebrity. I think it's cool.'

'Are you crazy, Driss?' asks Pollie. 'Do you want to be next?'

'They'll be writing about you in the paper before you know it,' says Lizzie.

'Thank you, ladies,' says Mia, 'but I'd like you to leave.'

'No,' snaps Pollie. '*You're* the one who's going to leave.'

'Leave me alone!' shouts Mia.

She steps forward and her neighbours take flight. Pollie is so startled that she drops her copy of *The Healthy Mind*. The newspaper lands on the top step.

Vigilance Required

Mens Sana: The Healthy Mind, Monday 14 July

Heinrich Kramer appeals for civil vigilance in response to heightened terrorist threat

Optimism is a virtue, but virtue alone is not enough to protect our society from the rising tide of terrorism. This is the lesson that should be learned from the announcement last night that further strikes are on the way.

Radicalised resistance groups pose a serious threat to our society, a threat that is growing by the day. The time has come for our politicians and media to face the truth, no matter how painful it may be. We can no longer ignore the fact that certain individuals – people who appear to lead entirely normal lives – are prepared to wage war on the Method and therefore against the citizens of this state. Tomorrow's terrorist could be an apparently harmless acquaintance, neighbour, colleague or friend. These people do not conform to a single demographic or socio-economic profile; they disguise themselves in all walks of life. Method Defence holds detailed information on the operational resources, communication lines and planned activities of key PRI cells, but the wider network of sympathisers, lone fanatics and independent resistance groups is all but impossible to monitor and control.

The authorities are reluctant to release detailed information until measures are in place to neutralise the threat. Reliable sources believe the next strike is likely to involve biological weapons. Possible targets include the purification plants for air and water, which could be hijacked by terrorists seeking to perpetrate a bacterial or viral attack.

Given the information blackout, we can only speculate about the identity of the individuals behind the threat. According to experts, the campaign of violence may well be linked to twenty-seven-year-old Moritz Holl, who was under investigation by Method Defence in the run-up to his death in May this year. The convicted murderer and rapist kicked up a media storm when he refused to accept responsibility for his crimes and subsequently eluded official justice by killing himself in prison. Readers of this paper will remember his oft-cited mantra, 'You are sacrificing me on the altar of your delusions', which anti-Method propagandists have adopted in their campaign.

The Healthy Mind has since learned that Moritz Holl's childhood was blighted by illness. 'He thought nobody understood him − our parents, his friends, me,' said his sister, Mia Holl. 'He talked more to plants and animals than to us.' This latest information confirms the view of Moritz Holl as an enemy combatant, and the new wave of PRI violence is doubtless connected to his death.

'It's not a question of *if* but *when* the terrorists will use a dirty bomb,' said the Minister for Security at a press conference this morning. For now, the authorities are doing their best to guarantee the safety of every citizen, but they need *your* help. Civil vigilance is imperative. Our system is devoted to the well-being of its citizens, but we cannot allow its trusting, optimistic outlook to blind us to the threat. We are all responsible for Method Defence.

Citizens, be vigilant!

Hedge-riding

The ideal inamorata reads the article to Mia and intones the words in a gentle voice. From her lips, Kramer's tirade sounds like a verse from an epic poem. Mia, who is back on her stationary bike, takes a break from her furious campaign against the missing final kilometres and applauds.

'Bravo! Bravo! What a triumph of journalism! *"He thought nobody understood him – our parents, his friends, me," said his sister, Mia Holl.* It's absolute genius!'

'I've never read such contemptible lies,' says the ideal inamorata, red spots of anger blooming on her cheeks.

'The world is full of contemptible lies,' says Mia. 'Just look at any newspaper.'

'Weren't you listening, Mia? Don't you realise what he's doing?'

'Sure. He's mobilising the troops in the war against anti-Method agitators.'

'No, he's preparing the charge sheet against Mia Holl!'

'You're just paranoid.' Mia is pedalling again; she suddenly ups the tempo. 'It's pretty funny, come to think of it. A delusion with delusions.'

'You still don't get it, do you? He's publicly accusing

Moritz of terrorism and he cited you by name. You're not anonymous any more. You need to *do* something!'

'On the contrary,' says Mia. 'While I'm here, racking up virtual kilometres on an exercise bike, the world is turning around me, spinning backwards and forwards towards an unknown goal. The situation is bad enough without my doing something.'

'You want everything to be harmless, don't you, Mia? Your brother was just a big kid; Kramer is a starry-eyed dreamer. And you're a perfectly innocent citizen on a stationary bike. The fact is, you're a coward. All your rationalising, your pros and cons, your knowing better and knowing best serves a single purpose: it gives you licence to shrug your shoulders for the rest of your life.'

'Nobody ever died from a shrug of the shoulders, but the world has gone under on countless occasions because of heroism, martyrdom and ideas. Would you rather I leaned out of the window, proclaimed a revolution and called for Kramer's head?'

'You could give it a try.'

'Enough!' It is clear from Mia's tone that she is furious. 'I'm sick of your empty words!'

'Empty words?' The ideal inamorata almost chokes and has to take a few breaths to calm herself down. 'How's this for substance? Step one – you accept that Moritz was a victim of the Method and your friend Kramer was involved. Step two – you repeat after me: The Method demonstrated its fundamental injustice by killing my brother. Step three – you call Rosentreter. Step four – you sue Kramer for libel. Step five – you find an open-minded journalist and set the story—'

'Wow,' says Mia sarcastically. 'Heinrich Kramer must be shaking in his boots. What a stunning plan, my beloved inamorata. It combines the pointlessness of human endeavour with the absurdity of bothering to try.'

'Listen to yourself. You're picking holes in the final stages of the strategy before you've considered steps one and two. You're scared, Mia Holl. Go ahead and take the first two steps, stick up for your brother. Then it won't seem so absurd.'

Mia is cut to the quick. Sometimes a person can be right in such a fundamental way that an answer is superfluous. It puts an end to the never-ending cycle of on-the-one-hand, on-the-other-hand. It ushers in an almost blissful calm. Mia looks at the pedals and watches her feet going up and down. For a few seconds, she thinks of nothing.

'Do you know what a hægtesse is, Mia?'

Mia looks up in surprise. It takes an effort of concentration to focus on the unknown word.

'It's an old term for witch,' says the ideal inamorata.

'A witch,' echoes Mia. 'Witches rode broomsticks. They were hunchbacked old hags who ended up in the oven or being burnt at the stake.'

'Hægtesse derives from the same word as hedge. A witch is a hedge spirit. She doesn't ride a broomstick, she rides the hedge.'

'Why are you telling me this?'

'The hedge is a boundary, Mia. A witch rides the boundary between the civilised world and the wild world beyond. She straddles this world and the next, life and death, body and mind. She rides the line between yes and no, faith and atheism. She doesn't take sides; the *between* is her realm. Does that remind you of anyone?'

Mia doesn't reply. She gets off the bike and walks to the window. Outside, a bird is fluttering around the flowerpots, pecking disappointedly at the artificial flowers. It looks at Mia reproachfully before flying away.

'People who don't take sides,' says the ideal inamorata, 'are outsiders. And outsiders live dangerously. Every now and then the authorities like to demonstrate their power by making an example. It happens a lot when people are losing faith. Outsiders are good targets because they don't know what they want. They hang on a silken thread, ready to fall.'

'I'm not an outsider,' says Mia weakly.

'Deep down you don't see the point of spending time with other people. As far as I'm aware, you've only made two exceptions, one of whom is dead and the other your enemy. It's enough to make you not belong.'

The outer Mia frowns and pretends not to follow, while the inner Mia accepts that the ideal inamorata is right. She understands the seriousness of the problem. The Method is based on the health of its citizens, and health is the norm. But what is normal? Normal is that which already exists, the prevailing condition. But normal is also normative — an expectation, the thing to be wished for. The norm is a double-edged sword. A person can be measured against that which exists, in which case she will be found to be normal and healthy, therefore good. Or a person can be measured against an expectation and found to be wanting. The norm can be changed at will. For those on the inside, the double-edged sword is a defensive weapon. For outsiders, it's a terrifying threat. It has the power to make you ill.

When Mia enters a public space – a department store, a high-speed train, her place of work or any other shared area – she never has the feeling that she is coming home. She doesn't burst through the door, shout 'hello', clap everyone on the shoulder and sit herself down on the comfiest chair. Most of the time she tries to go unnoticed. Some days she listens at the door to make quite certain before leaving the apartment that no one is outside. She needs time and space for herself and her thoughts. After work, she goes home instead of joining in with group activities. In the evening, she would rather sit on her stationary bike than on the management board of a local sports club. She talks to an invisible woman, not a best friend or a husband.

The ideal inamorata is trying to suggest that Mia is exactly like Moritz, save in one regard: Mia hides her difference by conforming to the system, whereas Moritz wore it like a badge. No one would ever describe Mia as 'abnormal', but no one calls her 'normal' either. She rides the hedge.

'Are you trying to warn me?' she asks.

The ideal inamorata nods wordlessly.

'It's sweet of you,' says Mia, 'but there's really no need. I'm not naive enough to think we can choose our place in life. At most we bring the nails and timber; others build the frame.'

'There's always a decision to be made,' says the ideal

inamorata. 'Do you want to be a perpetrator — or a victim?'

Mia's answer makes the ideal inamorata bury her head in her hands despairingly.

'I find both options decidedly unappealing,' she says.

Pointed Horns: Part II

'Of course they're unappealing,' said Moritz. 'That's why I've decided to be neither. It's a principle of mine.'

They were sitting by the river, Mia with her shoes and socks off and her trousers rolled up to the knees, which was her way of saying she was sorry. Their feet dangled casually in the water.

'By the way,' said Moritz, poking her gently in the ribs, 'I heard what you said last night when I was leaving.'

'That I'm your home?'

The rod dropped to the ground as Moritz grabbed Mia and hugged her tightly, so tightly she almost vanished in his embrace. It is humankind's greatest curse that the happiest moments in life can only be identified when they are over.

'Are you dealing with it all right?' asked Mia when he finally let go.

'I think so. You don't spend half your life studying philosophy only to be caught out by the phenomenon of death.'

Moritz raised a professorial index finger and assumed an expression that was probably supposed to convey that the old Moritz Holl had returned.

'We come from darkness and return to darkness. In between lie the experiences of life. But the beginning and the end, birth and death, we do not experience; they have no subjective character, they fall entirely in the category of objective events. And that's that,' he recited.

Mia laughed out loud. 'In other words, you live for yourself and die for others,' she said.

'That's the beauty of it,' replied Moritz. 'It would be disastrous the other way round. But remember, Mia: if you live for yourself, you need to swerve every now and then to avoid other people. You know what happens when you bump into others?'

'In your case, trouble, I shouldn't wonder.'

'It forces you to decide. The choice is always the same: betray yourself – or say what you think. The second option is dangerous.'

'It's nothing new,' said Mia impatiently. She didn't want to spoil the mood with a discussion about politics. 'You can't blame the Method.'

'That's not my point! It starts with the simplest things, like getting on a train. Maybe you feel like singing at the top of your voice or kissing the woman with all the shopping bags, or maybe you don't want to pay for a ticket because they're ridiculously over-priced. But in the end you buy a ticket, you don't sing, you sit down and you hide your face behind *The Healthy Mind*. I'd never join a group like the PRI – assuming it even exists. The problem would be exactly the same. I'd be forced to think, speak and act in a certain way. The only demand I make from life is the right to my own reality. In my mind, Sibylle isn't dead. In my mind, there is freedom. In my mind, people are dancing, drinking and partying in the streets, and the police are there too, watching and talking. The celebrations go through the night, and in the morning one of the neighbours complains about the noise. The officer gives him a bored look and drawls, "If you want something done about it, you should call the police."'

Moritz laughed, fished a cigarette out of his pocket and lit it. Mia frowned disapprovingly but didn't object.

'I don't want to argue with you,' she said, 'but aren't you dodging everyone else's reality by living your own?'

'Very true.' Moritz gripped the cigarette with his teeth and picked up his rod. 'A constant flickering, that's what freedom is for humans. Subjectivity, objectivity. Conformity, resistance. On, off. A free man is like a faulty bulb.'

Mia was about to reply when she heard rustling from the bushes. Looking up, she expected to see a deer or a great big bacteria with pointed horns. A uniformed officer stepped into the clearing. And another. And a third. Moritz was so shocked that he didn't think to throw the glimmering cigarette into the water. In the space of a second they had pulled him to his feet, twisted his arms behind his back and handcuffed his wrists.

'Moritz Holl,' said the first officer, 'I am arresting you on suspicion of the rape and murder of Sibylle Meiler.'

'You have the right to remain silent,' said the second. 'Anything you say may be taken down and used in evidence.'

'You have the right to consult a solicitor,' said the first.

'Let him go!' shouted Mia.

'If you want something done about it,' said Moritz, looking at his sister with desperate eyes, 'you should call the police.'

'I'm sorry for the inconvenience,' said the third.

The Right to Remain Silent

'And then he was gone,' says Mia to the river. 'Of all the things he missed in prison, he would have missed you most.'

She has taken off her shoes and socks, and her feet are dangling in the water. The grass beside her is unoccupied. She has kept up her weekly walk, even without Moritz. The route has become a road to Calvary with stations of the cross: the warning sign, the thicket, the trail. At the very end is the cathedral, erected from the river and the glade.

'He wouldn't have minded dying, if it meant seeing you again.'

Jealous, Mia slaps her bare feet against the water, creating a splash. The river, unmoved, continues to flow. Something rustles in the bushes, and Mia is so shocked that she doesn't think to cast the glimmering cigarette into the river. The stuff of nightmares steps into the clearing.

'Mia Holl,' says the first officer, 'I'm arresting you on suspicion of anti-Method activities and leading an anti-Method cell.'

Before Mia has time to realise what is happening, she

has been hauled to her feet with her arms twisted behind her back.

'Who were you meeting here?' says the second officer.

'You have the right to remain silent,' says the first.

The second tightens his grip until Mia yelps with pain. 'I asked you a question,' he barks. 'Who were you meeting here?'

'No one,' says Mia. 'I'd like to put on my shoes.'

'I apologise for any inconvenience,' says the third.

Mia's right hand is touching her back in a place that she had previously thought impossible. The thumb pressing against her larynx releases her from the obligation to scream. Pain causes white dots to spiral through her field of vision. The uniformed officers drag her out of the cathedral.

Exemption

More furniture has arrived, furniture and people. More tables, chairs and heavy desks, more black-robed mannequins and, for the first time since the start of Mia's trial, a handful of spectators. A team of journalists is unpacking its equipment. The room looks bigger than last time: the hearing has shifted to the central court. At the front of the room, Mia spots Sophie, the judge with the blonde ponytail and the nervous habit of putting her pencil in her mouth. The public prosecutor, Barker, is here as well, tilting back on his chair with his hands on the edge of his desk. The look on his face is disdainful; he has a state-sanctioned licence to know everything better than the rest of the world. Sitting in the front row of the public gallery is Kramer. His eyes are fixed on Mia and his gaze is intense, as if he has been missing her. From time to time he gives a little wave. The other familiar figure is Lutz Rosentreter, who turns up late, sits next to Mia and places a large stack of documents on the desk. He avoids eye contact with the others and seems strangely contented, as if he were focusing his attention on more enjoyable pursuits.

'That's Hutschneider,' he says softly, flicking through

his notes, 'the associate judge. On the other side, Judge Weber from the Federal Office for Method Defence, two lay judges, the clerk of the court and the court administrator. A doctor and security personnel to keep an eye on you. They've gone to an awful lot of trouble on your account; you should be honoured.'

Instead, Mia feels a mixture of fear and irrational excitement, as if she were five years old and it was the night before her birthday, for which a magnificent celebration has been planned. She wishes that her party dress were a little more comfortable. She is wearing overalls made of paper that rustle whenever she moves. The doctor comes over to spray her with disinfectant for the third time this morning. At the request of one of the lay judges, he scans the chip in her upper arm.

'Well,' says Rosentreter. 'This is it. No more mediation or meddlesome offers of help. Method Defence does things properly.'

'Where *were* you?' asks Mia. 'First I can't get rid of you and then you disappear. The court was on the point of assigning a new counsel.'

'I was doing some research – a fascinating case.'

'How nice to be able to continue your education.'

Rosentreter finally looks at Mia and beams at her brightly. He is impervious to sarcasm in his present state.

'The case is open,' declares Sophie. Her gaze takes in the room, sweeping over Mia as if she and Mia had never met and would never have reason to do so, least of all in their present roles. 'The relevant parties are present. Let the charges be read.'

Barker rises cumbersomely from his chair.

'Santé, ladies and gentlemen.' He knows the charges by heart, but he opens his file all the same. 'The defendant is charged with anti-Method activities and with spearheading an anti-Method faction. She is further charged with repeated misuse of toxic substances in the first degree. The prosecution calls attention to the following facts. First, the defendant is known to have made verbal attacks on the Method in private and public. According to the court's main witness, Heinrich Kramer, she expressly blames the Method for the death of her brother. The defendant has also made it perfectly clear that she rejects the authority of the state.' Barker leafs through his file. 'I quote: *I want to be left alone . . . I can deal with the fallout from the incident without the intervention of the Method and its associated institutions.*'

'Thank you, Barker,' interrupts Sophie. 'The judge is sufficiently acquainted with the defendant's utterances. She was there.'

'Second, the defendant was apprehended in a location known to Method Defence as a meeting point for suspected PRI sympathisers. According to the arresting officers, she was smoking a cigarette.'

'The defendant's recidivist tendencies are also known to the judge,' says Sophie with a cynicism that doesn't suit her.

'When asked to explain her presence at the aforementioned meeting point, the defendant stated she was meeting *no one*. The prosecution believes that *No one* is the code name of a PRI activist.'

'Pure conjecture,' says Rosentreter. 'I assume this is the prosecution's idea of a joke . . . ?'

'Be so kind as to wait your turn,' says Sophie. 'Next time you speak without permission, I'll assume you wish to leave the court.'

'The prosecution calls Heinrich Kramer to the stand,' says Barker. 'The prosecution also calls for the defendant to be interrogated about her political views.'

'Agreed,' says Sophie. 'Herr Rosentreter, what does the defence recommend?'

'An immediate suspension of the trial,' says Rosentreter. 'The matter should never have been brought to court.'

'You still want to pursue your application for exemption?' asks Sophie with almost amused astonishment.

'As a matter of fact, we're applying for the court to be recused on suspicion of bias.'

There is a murmur of excitement.

The judge looks at Rosentreter, who returns her gaze unflinchingly. She leans over to Hutschneider and Weber and a whispered debate ensues.

'Declined,' she says at last. 'The trial will continue. I advise the private counsel to consider his client's well-being and stick to the rules. Frau Holl, please rise for questioning.'

'Go on,' says Rosentreter to Mia, who has been listening to the proceedings with the bemusement of someone adrift in a foreign language. She stays seated until Rosentreter pokes her in the ribs; then she rises, rustles around the dock in her paper suit and sits at the little table in front of the judge's lectern.

'Do I have to take an oath?' she asks.

'You're not *entitled* to take an oath,' says Sophie. 'Oaths are reserved for witnesses. In future, you might want to look for a lawyer who can brief you on basic legal proced-ures. In the event that . . . you're arrested again.'

'Frau Holl, we'd like to confirm a few personal details,' says Barker.

'I'm a scientist,' says Mia, 'not a terrorist.'

There is laughter from the public gallery; the judge restores order with a threatening gesture.

'Come on, Frau Holl,' says Barker. 'It's not like you to hold back with your opinions. This is your chance. What do you think of our political system?'

'Science,' says Mia, 'broke up the long-standing marriage between humankind and the transcendental. The soul, progeny of this union, was given up for adoption. It left us with the body, which became our main concern. The body is temple and altar; our highest god, our greatest sacrifice; sacred and enslaved. Logically speaking, it was inevitable. Do you see what I mean?'

'No,' says Barker.

'Absolutely,' says Sophie. 'Please go on.'

'The sort of person who recognises the logical inevit-ability of a development is not the sort of person who swims against the tide. For such a person, swimming against the tide is pointless, futile. So you want to know what I think about anti-Method activities? The PRI? Revolution?' Mia is becoming animated. She rolls up the sleeves of her paper overalls. 'Revolution is when the many rise up against the few, the few being a handful of people who make the decisions at any one time. In all other respects, the few and the many are the same.'

She turns to Kramer as if her explanation were

intended for him alone. He lifts his chin and signals for her to face the judge.

'What would you think if you saw a pack of wolves attacking and killing its leader?' she says. 'You'd think it was natural, wouldn't you? You'd think it was nature's way of finding a new leader for the pack. It's that simple! We can talk about revolution, power and oppression, politics, the Method, economics, private interest and the common good, we can use a thousand new words for describing matters that seem complicated and important, but it all comes down to one thing: a human arrangement. Since the gods are no longer in the picture, it's irredeemably banal. A pack of wolves that get rid of their leader every few years.'

Barker shuffles in his seat. He looks like a loose collection of bones barely held together by his robe.

'I'm not sure the defendant's statement was intelligible to the court,' he says.

'On the contrary,' says Sophie. 'Frau Holl has made it clear that she can't see the sense in revolution, since revolution is a conflict between two groups of humans, and humans, as the court would agree, are identical in worth. The judge accepts the statement as admissible evidence.'

'Pardon me,' says Hutschneider, 'but in the same statement Frau Holl asserted that a pack, um, I mean, a society should replace its leader, or rather, its government every few years.'

'The point is,' says Mia, 'I want nothing to do with it. My brother accused me of supporting the Method only because I despised humankind. He was probably right, but it doesn't change the fact that I believe in the Method.'

'If the defendant's belief in the system is grounded in her contempt for humanity, it follows that she despises the state,' says Hutschneider craftily, jabbing the air with his pen as he speaks.

'Is this a courtroom or a debating club?' asks Barker, running his fingers around his collar as if he were overheating.

'First official caution,' says Sophie.

'The system teaches us to think rationally,' says Mia. 'Everything about me is rational. At school I was taught to approach every problem from at least two different sides. Logic splits everything into two opposing parts. At the end of the process, you get zero.'

'Ha, now I see where she's coming from,' exclaims Barker. 'Frau Holl is campaigning for freedom from *consequences*.'

'Logic makes me sit on the fence. I'm forever in between. I can't decide for or against: I'm not in the least bit dangerous.'

'I suspect the opposite is the case,' says Hutschneider darkly.

'Frau Holl,' says Sophie, and does something she has never done in court: she reaches back and unties her hair, 'in our previous conversations we talked about the connection between personal well-being and the common good. Can you explain your views to the court?'

'The state,' says Mia obediently, 'is there to serve humanity's natural desire for life and happiness. Power is legitimate only in so far as it serves this goal. The state must unite the well-being of the individual and the whole.'

'Many of us are working very hard to achieve precisely that,' says Sophie. 'We're doing well, I think you'd agree.'

'Maybe you are,' says Mia softly, 'but maybe it's not enough. Maybe for a system to be legitimate, it has to be infallible, which is humanly impossible, per se.'

'Did you hear that?' crows Barker. 'Now we've got her! Frau Holl is suggesting that errors in the interpretation of the Method would justify . . .' His voice cracks with excitement and he loses his thread. 'The prosecution demands—'

'Your Honour,' says Rosentreter, who has been sitting with his eyes half closed, showing no sign of whether he has actually been following the progress of the trial, 'the defence would like to lodge an application for evidence relating to the Moritz Holl verdict to be heard by the court, the material in question being relevant to the current case.'

Mia meets Sophie's eyes, and there is a moment of calm. In the fields beyond the city, mouldering fences topple over without a sound. The wind turbines stretch into the distance, rotating slowly and ponderously, as if the blades were turning the wind, not the other way round. And yet, thinks Mia, wind and wind alone is the reason for the light being on in the room while people interrogate each other about their political views. The world, Mia thinks, is a reflection on the outer surface of her mind. By the time the moment passes, she has forgotten the nature of Rosentreter's request. She hadn't understood it in the first place.

'Granted,' says Sophie.

Sophie has signed her professional death sentence. It is ironic that her reservations revolve around the likely reaction of Messrs Hutschneider and Weber. The associate judges will doubtless be furious with her decision. The introduction of new material will drag out the hearing and in any case it is common knowledge that this nice guy Rosentreter is way out of his depth. The case is politically sensitive, and the last thing Sophie needs is a floundering private counsel. All the same, she grants him his intermezzo. She has to. For one thing, it's the correct decision in procedural terms, since Moritz Holl features prominently in the arguments put forward by both prosecution and defence. Quite apart from that, Rosentreter has gone to a great deal of trouble. As he sits there, his desk covered with sheets of paper, sorting and re-sorting his documents as if weighing up where to begin, Sophie feels sorry for him. She mistakes his barely contained excitement for nerves.

In the same way that Rosentreter thinks of himself as nice and is held to be so by others, Sophie thinks of herself as good and is thought of as such. Part of being good is always striving to do everything just right. A good person will want to illuminate every aspect of a case, even if the defendant is irksome and Messrs Barker, Hutschneider and Weber will be late for their lunch. A good person will respect other people's hard work, even if the person in question perspires heavily, throws documents over the side of the desk, and fails to find the port for his memory key. With these thoughts in mind, thoughts that, incredibly, take no more than a fraction of a second to pass through the human brain, Sophie, who can't be held responsible for anything, marches to her doom.

At last Rosentreter finds the right slot for his memory key. Mia's face disappears from the screen to be replaced by Moritz: boyish, handsome, smiling mischievously, with, as they say, a roguish look in his eye. Mia, who isn't prepared for the picture, turns away and buries her face in her hands. Rosentreter raises his index finger; the image changes and a strange photograph lights up the courtroom. Pictured on the screen is a perfectly round, flat disc, under which various bean-shaped items are swimming. Their crooked bodies are a grainy black with white casing.

'Blood,' says Rosentreter, 'but not the standard variety.'

He raises his finger again. The next image shows a huge number of white bubbles and a reduced number of red ones. 'A high concentration of white blood cells. You can clearly see the leukocytes.'

'This had better be going somewhere,' says Barker. 'No one asked for a lesson in haematology.'

'Herr Rosentreter, kindly stick to the matter in hand,' says Hutschneider, glaring first at Rosentreter and then at the judge.

The screen changes to show a diagram with coloured squares and circles, all with three-letter acronyms: AML, ALL, CLL and other such combinations.

'Leukaemic cells proliferate in the bone marrow,' says Rosentreter. 'As the disease progresses, it is common for the liver, spleen and lymph nodes to be affected and their function impaired. At the age of six, Moritz Holl was found to be suffering from paleness, fatigue and pain in his bones. He also bruised easily.'

'His whole body was covered in bruises,' adds Mia. 'He looked like he'd been beaten black and blue.'

'Objection, Your Honour,' says Barker. 'I can't see why we should listen to this distasteful—'

'Bone marrow transplantation,' says Rosentreter determinedly. 'It's the usual treatment, together with monoclonal antibodies and various drugs.'

There is fidgeting and muttering in the courtroom, which Rosentreter assiduously ignores. The fact that the presiding judge is chewing on her pencil persuades him of the need to proceed at greater speed.

'The classic method of bone marrow transplantation uses stem cells from the bone marrow. In the past, finding compatible donors was extremely difficult. These days, thanks to the Method, every citizen's tissue type is listed in a database. This allows for mandatory anonymous donations of stem cells. We can say with pride that no one dies of leukaemia any more.'

'That's truly heartening,' says Sophie, 'but since none of this is relevant, you'll have to stop there.'

'Just a few more words,' says Rosentreter. 'The actual procedure is pretty basic. The donated material is transferred via a cannula to the recipient. The bone marrow finds its way into the bones and ten or so days later, it starts to generate new blood cells.'

'This is going too far!' exclaims Barker.

'We should call the court bailiff,' says Hutschneider.

'Or notify the Agency,' adds Weber.

'Your Honour,' calls Kramer from the public gallery, 'I strongly recommend you put an immediate halt to this performance!'

His voice cuts through the hubbub, resonating so sonorously that it seems to come not from him, but from the ceiling. The gallery falls silent. Kramer's commanding tone is strangely at odds with his bearing. He is sitting ramrod straight, with his hands on his knees. His face has paled and his mouth continues to move silently, as if he were explaining the situation to himself. He looks like a man who, for the first time in his life, has been overtaken by events. Yet Kramer is the only person in the room who knows where Rosentreter is heading; he knows what the lawyer has found. He and Mia look at each other. Right now, his silent lips might whisper, *The system is human. Of course it is flawed.*

'Herr Kramer,' says Sophie, 'you are not a member of this court and you have no right to comment.'

If the proverbial pin were to drop now, it would be heard by everybody in the room. Even Rosentreter has frozen in front of the screen; his next sentence is trapped in his throat.

'Please accept my apologies,' says Kramer. 'Unfortunately, circumstances compel me to—'

As Kramer rises to his feet, Rosentreter comes back to life.

'After the transplant, the patient's blood group will match the donor's,' he says with the urgency of a marked man whose only chance of escape is speed. 'Their immune system will match and so will—'

'Rosentreter!' shouts Kramer.

'—their DNA!'

The defence counsel raises an arm as if to banish Kramer to his seat with the power of the occult. The image on the screen changes. We see the face of an unknown man, approximately fifty years of age, head shaven and skin lined with deep wrinkles that make the photograph look like a drawing.

'This,' says Rosentreter, 'is Walter Hannemann, the probable murderer of Sibylle Meiler. He was Moritz Holl's donor.'

'I knew it, Moritz!' shouts Mia, looking up to the ceiling. 'Please believe me, Moritz! I knew it all along!'

The situation breaks into its constituent parts. Barker leaves his desk, grabs Rosentreter by the sleeve and talks furiously at him without stopping. The security personnel, overwhelmed by the chaos, grab Mia by the shoulders, while Hutschneider yells frantically into his phone. The spectators leave the gallery, led by the journalists, shouting over each other in preparation for the briefing with Mia Holl. In the fields beyond the city, the turbine blades turn ponderously in the changing wind. In the midst of the tumult, Kramer is slumped on the bench, inspecting his cuticles and smoothing his already immaculate hair. Sophie, whose blonde hair is draped loose about her shoulders, makes no attempt to hide her face, even though tears are flowing down her cheeks. An alkaline salty solution, thinks Mia, watching attentively as Sophie continues to cry. A fluid secreted from our glands when the body is subjected to the shock of pain – physical or emotional. It also contains traces of mucin and protein, as we have learned elsewhere.

'Sophie,' says Mia, 'it is not your fault.'

It is impossible to tell if the judge hears Mia above the noise. They will never see each other again.

That's Our Mia

Driss has bounded up the steps with giant strides and jammed her finger against the buzzer on Lizzie's door. She doesn't let go until someone opens. It isn't Lizzie, it's Pollie. She stands there, pale-faced, as if she has seen a ghost.

'Quick, turn on the television!' Driss is still speaking when she notices the noise. The television is on already, in every single room of Lizzie's flat.

'Stem cells,' says Pollie. 'Legal scandal. Can't make head nor tail of it.'

'Because you're thick!' shouts Lizzie from the kitchen. 'The courts, the police . . . You can no longer count on anything.'

'Look, there's Mia!' Driss is still standing in the doorway, apparently rooted to the spot. She points to the pictures on the screen. Mia's face is about to vanish behind the microphones.

'She didn't do anything wrong, I knew it!' Impatiently, Driss fends off Pollie, who is trying to pull her inside. 'I was the only one who did!'

'Frau Holl,' says the voice of a reporter, 'were you surprised by this morning's revelations?'

'He was my brother. I knew him.'

'Frau Holl, how are you feeling right now?'

'I'm ashamed of myself. I believed in his innocence, but maybe not strongly enough.'

'What do you mean by that?'

'I believed he was innocent, but I failed to draw any wider conclusions.'

'Frau Holl, the Method is responsible for a gross miscarriage of justice. Is it still a legitimate system, in your view?'

'I'm not going to answer that . . .' says Mia.

'Did you hear that, girls? She's not going to answer!' calls Lizzie across the hallway.

'. . . but it's a question I'll *ask* myself every day.'

'That's our Mia!' says Driss.

And here comes Mia in person. She is coming up the steps with Rosentreter. She is wearing normal clothes again, and she is staring at her feet.

'Mia,' says Driss as the pair reach the landing, 'we're so sorry.'

'*She's* so sorry,' says Pollie.

'Don't look at me!' yells Mia. 'You'll get the plague! Tuberculosis, cholera, leukaemia!'

Pollie reaches out and yanks Driss into the apartment. The door slams shut.

'This way,' says Rosentreter. 'Up the stairs.'

Maximal Triumph

'That,' says Rosentreter, 'was what you might call a maximal triumph!'

Rosentreter cracks open a bottle of contraband champagne. He is celebrating a historic moment, the overture to a magnificent political oratorio, and whether or not he hears the oratorio, he wants to revel in the overture and savour the unforgettable beauty of its parts – the dull roll of the timpani, the heartbeat of a system on the verge of collapse; soaring trumpets, the media hitting previously unattainable notes; the soothing tones of the harp, political assurances and promises; and the frenetic playing of the string section, public opinion.

'You know the best bit? The first violin is absolutely silent!' Rosentreter laughs and slaps his thigh in delight. Then he fills two tumblers with champagne.

Mia is standing at the window and watching as the night sky works itself up for a summer storm above the city. She feels like a passenger who, after days of waiting on the platform and peering into the hazy distance, has finally seen the train arrive – from the other direction. The champagne poured for her by Rosentreter is gradually getting warmer in her hands.

The defence counsel's glass is already half empty; the champagne lifts him like a magic carpet. Rosentreter is no more accustomed to alcohol than to courtroom success. He never shone as a student; his good grades testified to the fact that his professors liked him, not that he was suited to the law. He has waited half his life for this moment. Even so, Rosentreter has no intention of losing his head over this. Granted his picture is being beamed into every living room in the country, and he could step outside onto Mia's roof garden and address the excited crowds. But Rosentreter is smart enough to know that Fortune tends to favour the strongest, which makes her an unreliable friend.

'A good composer,' he says, 'follows the boldness of the overture with a peaceful first movement. We'll lie low for a while. Plan the next move carefully. I like to work in the background, always have done. Santé!'

'Santé,' says the ideal inamorata, swigging from the bottle behind his back.

Mia hasn't been listening to the overture; Mia is watching the storm. The street is lit on one side only, so the shadows of the trees lurch drunkenly across the apartments in the opposite block. They seem to clutch at each other's hands as they stumble along. The wind gusts through every aperture in the building, riding on open doors and riffling through documents on desks. It rattles the blinds like castanets, fills the swings and see-saws with invisible children bobbing crazily up and down, and applauds itself with a sheet of tarpaulin on some scaffolding. On the rooftops, everything is banging and clattering as if a group of gods were playing skittles up above. Where are the people? The storm has driven them inside where they lie in their bedrooms, trying to sleep like animals in crates, doing their best to ignore the rumbling and roaring of nature, tortured by their awareness of the insignificance of their tiny, puffed-up lives in the *pas de deux* between the city and the sky. Human beings aren't part of the game; they aren't even spectators. At most they're dead leaves, swept aside and abandoned in the gutter.

'No interviews,' stipulates Rosentreter. 'No TV appearances. Keep yourself out of the public eye. That's why there are delivery companies, couriers and telecommunications. Stay indoors! Mia, are you listening to me?'

He reaches in vain for the champagne bottle, which the ideal inamorata has moved to the left.

'You should be celebrating,' says the ideal inamorata. 'I know your lawyer talks too much, but he's actually talking sense.'

The storm has reached the turbines; they spin faster and faster, the blades appear to evanesce. Mia imagines the thrum becoming louder, swelling to a roar, and the turbines lifting off the ground, a formation of a thousand aeroplanes, with only their propellers in sight. They lift their noses towards the sky and make a steep ascent, pulling the city with them.

'From now on,' says Mia slowly, '*his* name negates all reason. From now on, I'll do everything for love and free from fear.'

'I beg your pardon,' says the ideal inamorata.

'I've finally understood what you've been saying all this time. It's not enough to *believe* someone. It's not even enough to *know* they're innocent. It's about professing your loyalty.'

'Exactly,' says the ideal inamorata. 'Now come here and have a drink.'

'Listen,' says Mia.

'I'm listening,' says Rosentreter with a tipsy smile. This is his first taste of alcohol.

'Mia,' says the ideal inamorata, 'you haven't been yourself for weeks and now you're too much like you.'

'I mean, *really* listen.' At last Mia turns away from the window, takes a step into the room and looks at the ideal inamorata. 'The Method,' she quotes, 'demonstrated its fundamental injustice by killing my brother – step two.'

'True,' says Rosentreter as the ideal inamorata lowers her eyes to the floor, 'but we need to move carefully.'

'Step three – I'll call someone. But it won't be him.' She laughs in Rosentreter's face. 'He's here already. Step four – compose a broadside. Step five – publish it.'

'Mia,' pleads the ideal inamorata, 'take a moment to think things through.'

'Dear heart, you were the one who wanted me to do something. You wanted a flagship, a figurehead.'

'Mia,' says Rosentreter cautiously, 'who are you talking to?'

'I've got the plague,' says Mia, smiling. 'Leprosy, cholera. I'm ill. I'm free.'

Rosentreter rubs his nose with the back of his hand. 'You're not ill,' he says.

'From now on I won't turn round when I hear my name.'

'We mustn't let them harm you. We need you intact.'

As Mia walks towards Rosentreter, something lurks in her eyes that makes him shrink away.

'I don't need either of you,' she says. 'Get out of my apartment.'

'Mia,' says the ideal inamorata, 'Moritz wouldn't have wanted this.'

Mia hesitates for a moment. Her eyes scan the room.

'Are you sure?' she asks. 'Really sure?'

The ideal inamorata says nothing. Mia picks up her glass and throws its contents at Rosentreter's chest.

'Leave,' she says. 'Take the alcoholic stench of your triumph and parade it through the streets! If you don't want to meet the first violin, you'll have to hurry . . .'

Rosentreter doesn't move. Champagne is dripping from his suit. He wraps his jacket around his chest as if he were cold, takes a few steps back, turns and walks to the door. Mia watches him go, her hand resting on the ideal inamorata's shoulder.

'Do you want to know the truth?' says the ideal inamorata. 'You're finished; you're finished either way – which is exactly what you want.'

'The truth,' says Mia, 'is only visible from the corner of one's eye. The moment you look at it squarely, it becomes a lie.' She picks up the phone and taps in a number. 'Put me through to Heinrich Kramer.'

The Second Category

'I was wondering how you felt about it.'

'About what?'

'Life.'

Mia is boiling some water in the kitchen. She gets out two cups and cuts a few slices of lemon. She looks briefly into the living room as if to satisfy herself that her guest hasn't left.

'Oh,' says Kramer. 'Very neat. Really.'

He is sitting on the sofa beside the ideal inamorata, and he is back to his usual self. His cheeks are neither pallid nor flushed and his hands are out of his pockets. The awkward situation he got into in the courtroom will haunt him for the rest of his life.

He sees Mia looking at him, and smiles. 'I have a beautiful wife with long brown hair and two lovely children who cling to my legs and shout "Daddy!" as soon as I walk through the door.'

'Sounds wonderful.'

'It *is* wonderful. A centuries-old arrangement. In our personal relations, we've lived with the same basic model for thousands of years. Humans are programmed for a limited range of modes: love, hatred, fear, happiness, trust . . .'

'Revenge . . .'

'Yes, revenge, too. If you think about it, human existence is very simple. Happiness is a case in point. There are two basic categories for describing experience: positive, which means beneficial or propitious; or negative, which means disadvantageous or harmful. The key to happiness lies in filling one's life with experiences from the first category and avoiding the second.'

'It certainly sounds convincing.'

'It is. And how are you? Why don't you tell me about your life? Where's your husband? Where are your children?'

'I ask the questions,' says Mia, coming in from the kitchen and applying herself to serving two cups of water in an unconditional and perfect way. 'You can turn the screws on me, but I'd advise you to be careful: my brother is dead, and your conscience is a dog that wants to lick my hand.'

'I don't have a conscience, Frau Holl.'

'No, but you understand political necessity, which amounts to the same.'

'Very good,' says Kramer, laughing. 'You're learning to use your weapons.'

'How does it feel to be on the receiving end?'

'An experience from the second category, I'm afraid.' Kramer sips his water carefully. 'Yesterday, before your acquittal, a group of protesters gathered outside the courthouse. There weren't many of them – somewhere in the region of a hundred, according to the police. Still, the Method isn't keen on such gatherings.'

'And yet your colleagues are flirting with my case.'

'The majority of them, yes. Even supposedly like-minded journalists . . . You know Herr Wörmer from *What We All Think*?'

'What of him?'

'I suppose you could call him a protégé of mine. Anyway, Herr Wörmer took it upon himself to suggest that the value of a political system might lie in its ability to adjust to new developments, to arrange itself around the situation like a well-fitting coat. According to him, legitimate governments are like custom-made shoes that never pinch or rub. As if Wörmer knew the first thing about footwear! All of a sudden my colleagues are scrambling over each other to criticise the system.'

'You're not tempted to convert?'

'Don't insult me, Frau Holl. Accuse me of whatever you like, but not of opportunism.'

'Spoken like a true fanatic.'

'Spoken like a man of honour. I'm not interested in adjusting the system, and I don't give a damn about footwear or coats. The situation has taken an unfavourable turn. I'm ready to fight to the last drop of blood, as they used to say in the good old days.'

'There's one thing I don't understand,' says Mia. 'I can still hear you telling me that the human condition is a pitch-black room in which we crawl around like newborn babies. Why are you intent on spilling blood? The last drop, indeed?'

'I'm a believer, Mia, and this is my crusade. I believe in a political right to good health, derived from our inborn will to live. I believe that a system can only ever be just if it takes the body as its starting point. I believe that all men are equal in *body*, not in mind. Most of all, the Method's vision of humanity is superior to all that came before.'

Mia watches as Kramer settles into the pose of an orator. He presses his chin to his chest, encourages his eyebrows to rise up and down expressively, and shifts his weight in order to gesticulate freely with his right arm.

'Take a look at the history books,' he says. 'You'll see what happens when humans become infatuated with their physical ills. Barely fifty years ago, children were proud of scraped knees. Fully grown men and women drew hearts on each other's plaster casts. Everyone complained about hay fever, back pain and indigestion, when all they wanted was attention – *undeserved* attention. Physical suffering was a serious topic of conversation. A visit to the doctor's became a national sport. Illness was proof of one's existence, as if people had to suffer to know they were alive. For centuries, people worshipped weakness; it even became the basis of a world religion. People knelt before pictures of an anorexic, bearded masochist with barbed wire on his head and blood flowing down his cheeks. The pride of the sick, the sanctity of the sick, the narcissism of the sick; these were the vices that poisoned humanity from the inside.'

'Life,' says Mia breezily, 'begins at the height of its power. From birth, it's a steady decline towards the end. The dramaturgy is all wrong.'

'*D'accord.* But in modern society, rather than worship the error, we correct it: we've identified the problem, and there's no going back. How could anyone in this day and age argue rationally against seeing good health as the norm? Optimal functionality without weakness or impairment – health is the only possible ideal.'

'Bravo, Kramer.' Mia smiles like a contented cat and takes a sip of hot water. 'If my hands were free, I'd applaud. Kramer number 1 is an excellent demagogue, but Kramer number 2 thinks any given system is as good as the next. First we called it Christianity, then democracy, and now we call it the Method. Always claiming an absolute truth, always wanting absolute Good, and always foisting itself on the rest of the world. It's all religion. Why would an unbeliever like you want to fight in defence of the latest manifestation of the same old mistake?'

'Very sharp – but be careful not to cut yourself, Frau Holl. Shall I save you the trouble of dissecting me further and give you an honest response?'

Kramer abandons his orator's pose, rests his elbows on his knees and turns his palms towards the ceiling. He looks like a person trying to look like a person speaking from the heart. 'In all honesty,' he says, 'I despise the antiquated inheritance of the bourgeois Enlightenment, the backwardness of libertarian thought. I can't abide the childish pride of political partisans who insist on playing the hero. The people who complain about authority are simply too stupid, lazy or arrogant to appropriate the power they need to be effective. They stand on the sidelines and holler about injustice because they see the world as one big sour grape. But offer one of these self-declared revolutionaries a position of authority within the hated edifice, and I guarantee he'll shut up and get on with the job. What does it tell us about our fellow humans, Frau Holl? They're only too happy to claim that black is white when it plays to their vanity.'

'Well, well,' says Mia, smiling more broadly. 'It's astonishing how certain generalisations acquire a personal cast.'

'The impetus for progress,' says Kramer, ignoring Mia's last remark, 'comes from two things: society's hubris and the individual's need to prove himself. Every epoch in human history has claimed hundreds of thousands, if not millions of victims because people can't resolve themselves to settle for the status quo. The Method is a perfectly good system; there's no need to replace it with anything else.'

'Surely you're not serious? After everything that's happened.'

'Come on, Mia, you're not that petty. A personal tragedy doesn't make a political crisis. Every form of government claims the odd casualty, as I'm sure you're aware. Despite what happened to your brother, the Method is far and away the fairest, most reliable system in history. Why are you looking at me so fiercely? Surely you don't believe in a political paradise on Earth?'

'I'm not looking at you fiercely,' says Mia. 'I'm just intrigued. By the way, I'm at a slight advantage: I've given up on reason. I've learned to think with my heart.'

'How sweet! I didn't have you down as a sensitive girl. You've changed, Mia. I don't know whether I should be sorry or pleased. A few days ago, I almost thought we were kindred spirits.'

'I'd be honoured to have as little in common with you as possible.'

'As you like. But maybe you'd care to tell me what your newly discovered heart is thinking?'

'It's thinking about freedom.'

Kramer presses an index finger to his temple and groans.

'I didn't mean to give you a headache,' says Mia, 'but don't worry, you passed.'

'Passed what?'

'The test.' Mia arches her back and stretches luxuriantly. 'Would you like the results? You have recognised that you're intelligent – too intelligent to make binding, final and irreversible decisions. In other words, your intelligence debars you from power. Which is why you've nailed your pride and your sense of self-worth to the Method. You're a partisan, too, Herr Kramer. A partisan on the side of the status quo. It makes you an absolutely reliable enemy of mine.'

'I don't think you'll be short of enemies in future.'

'In that case, you should count yourself lucky that I decided to talk to *you*; I'm sure you'll be able to find a place for this episode in the chronicle of your importance. For my part, I only want you as my mouthpiece. You'll need a pen and paper. I'm relying on you as a man of honour to cite me directly.'

Kramer roars with laughter, then falls silent. He opens his mouth, starts to say something, and stops. For a few seconds it seems as though he might lose his self-control. The look that he bestows on Mia betrays a readiness to use physical violence. Little by little, the threat melts into a mocking grin, and Kramer lowers his head.

'Second category?' enquires Mia solicitously.

'Second category,' says Kramer, looking for paper and pen.

'My apologies, Mia,' says the ideal inamorata. 'Moritz would have loved this.'

The Nature of the Question

I refuse to trust a society that is made up of humans and based on a fear of what is human. I refuse to trust a civilisation that has sold out the mind to the body. I refuse to trust a body that represents a collective vision of a normalised body rather than my own flesh, my own blood. I refuse to trust a definition of normality based on good health. I refuse to trust a definition of health based on normality. I refuse to trust a system of government based on logical fallacies. I refuse to trust an idea of safety that claims to be the definitive answer without disclosing what the question is. I refuse to trust a philosophical system that holds existential debate to be over and done with. I refuse to trust an ethical framework that opts for 'functional' and 'non-functional' rather than confronting the paradox of good and evil. I refuse to trust a legal system that derives its success from controlling every aspect of its citizens' lives. I refuse to trust a population that believes total transparency exposes only those with something to hide. I refuse to trust the Method for valuing a person's DNA over his word. I refuse to trust the common good for seeing individuality as an unjustifiable expense. I refuse to trust personal interest that is merely a variation on a collective theme. I refuse to trust a political system that draws its popularity entirely from the promise of a life free of risk. I refuse to trust natural sciences that repudiate free will. I refuse to trust a notion of love that casts itself as the product of two optimally suited immune systems. I refuse to trust parents who see tree houses as accidents waiting to happen and pets as carriers of disease. I refuse to trust a system that claims to know better than I do what is good for me. I refuse to trust the person who took down the sign at the gates to humanity that said: 'Caution! Life leads to death!'

I refuse to trust myself because my brother had to die before I finally understood what it means to be alive.

A Matter of Trust

Kramer is feeling euphoric. He puts away his pen and paper and thanks Mia for her assistance in promoting the common cause. He is grateful to her, he says, for entrusting to him a political weapon of mass destruction, and he knows she can count on him to put it to good use. When Mia asks what he means by *common cause*, he looks at her in astonishment: has she not realised that fate has brought the two of them together to undertake a joint mission of an unspecified nature? She would agree, would she not, that any system of government should assure itself periodically of its mandate to rule? And isn't it time for the Method to test itself? To put the matter to a vote of confidence? In previous eras, governments struggling to assert their authority would call on parliament to dismiss them or come out in their support — isn't this exactly the situation facing the Method? And perhaps Mia, by publicising her views on the system, could contribute towards securing the right result? In any case, he likes her apartment and hopes she was comfortable there.

As Mia shows him to the door, she wonders why he spoke of her apartment in the past tense. Should she think of her efforts as belonging to the first or the second category? On what basis should the category be decided? Whose perspective should she apply? When the door shuts behind him, she ceases to care.

Now she is lying in the arms of the ideal inamorata and drinking from the champagne bottle that Rosentreter left behind. Suddenly the ideal inamorata starts talking in the past tense as well.

'I was moored on your shores for a while,' she says. 'You should be glad.'

'I wasn't friends with you; I was friends with your simulacrum,' says Mia.

'You're being cynical.'

'I'm being precise. I couldn't love you properly – not the way that Moritz did. It's always been hard to believe in your existence.'

'You won't have to any more.'

'You're leaving me, are you? Why?' Mia passes her the bottle. She strokes the ideal inamorata's forehead. The ideal inamorata keeps quiet. Her foot is tapping in time with a song that no one else can hear.

'I've achieved my goal,' she says at last. 'Moritz's final wish was for you to believe him, for you to understand what happened. For you to think of him in the right way.'

'Do you know what I told him? *I want to be the ground that trembles beneath your feet when the vengeance of the gods is visited upon you.* Fate likes us to keep our promises, I suppose.'

'I didn't think it would be this hard for me to leave you.' The ideal inamorata runs her hand lightly through Mia's hair. 'I'm concerned for you, Mia.'

'You needn't worry: technically, I'm a saint.'

'Martyrdom comes before sainthood.'

'I was never much interested in getting old – who wants to spend their time waiting for the next meal? Oh, come on!' she says as the ideal inamorata withdraws her hand. 'I was joking!'

'I don't have a sense of humour. There is no sentence so foolish that a human couldn't say it in all seriousness.'

Mia pulls the ideal inamorata towards her and kisses her on the lips. 'We have no idea how many times a day the world avoids the apocalypse. When you see Moritz, tell him I love him. Or rather, tell him that a tree house is for pulling up the ladder, eating cherries until your stomach hurts, getting birds' mess in your hair and still never wanting to come down. Will you tell him?'

'I promise.'

Mia takes a deep breath as if she is about to start a long sentence that will reveal the answer to everything, but her mouth is open because she needs to yawn. In no time she is asleep.

Cushion

She wakes to the noise of Method Defence breaking down her front door. Method Defence has no shortage of highly trained lock pickers with the ability to enter any building silently in a matter of seconds. When these people force their way into an apartment, they do so by choice. Three men storm into Mia's living room: a small army, driven forward by the momentum of their attack. Mia is lying on the couch; she has only just opened her eyes. She stares, bewildered, at the invaders. In her arms is not the ideal inamorata, but a cushion.

She kicks the first invader in the stomach. The second she attacks with raised claws, aiming for his face. The nail of her index finger goes deep under the lower lid of his right eye. None of these men grasp that Mia isn't protecting herself; she is defending the cushion with the ruthlessness of a lioness fighting for her newborn cub. The third manages to catch hold of her legs. Mia rears up and sinks her teeth into his neck, letting go only when she tastes blood. He cries out and smashes his fist into her forehead; she drops onto the sofa, dazed but not ready to surrender.

Not a word is spoken. There is no *sorry to disturb you* or *please forgive the inconvenience.* Mia's living room isn't the site of an arrest. This is a war, and maximum damage must be inflicted on the aggressors before they drag away their prey.

'Rapists! Thieves!'

'Marching in here with their dirty boots!'

'Don't be ridiculous, children! Look at their uniforms! It's the Agency.'

The commotion can be heard throughout the building. It draws the neighbours in their dressing gowns up the stairs to Mia's open door. On the other side of the door frame, a Method Defender has taken out a syringe and is waiting for his colleagues to restrain the demented woman. Blood is streaming from his nose and he sways unsteadily.

'They're taking Mia away.'

'There must be some mistake.'

'Mia is a heroine! It was in the papers!'

'Frau Holl is our most cherished resident.'

Despite limited vision through his swollen right eye, the Method Defender sees his opportunity and acts. The syringe comes down into Mia's upper arm.

'No!'

'It's their job, Driss.'

'It's not our place to get involved.'

'Driss, come back!'

Only when Mia's body slackens are the Method Defenders able to tear the cushion from her grasp. The man with the bloody nose tosses aside the syringe and kicks the cushion. When the willowy Driss throws herself against him, he brushes her off with one hand. Driss collides with the door frame and sinks to the floor. The uniformed men step over her as they carry Mia away from the apartment.

Statue of Liberty

'Dynamite!' says Rosentreter.

'Did you bring the mirror?'

Rosentreter rummages in his briefcase and pulls out a compact mirror. Mia leans towards the Plexiglas to examine her reflection. She is dressed in white paper overalls again. A large bruise adorns her forehead. Her lower lip is swollen, and one of her eyes looks red. In the mirror she catches the gaze of someone she knows. It isn't hers, so it probably belongs to Moritz.

'Great,' says Mia. 'Paper overalls, solitary confinement, a battered face. I couldn't get closer to my brother than this.'

Rosentreter quickly puts away the mirror. 'Your proclamation was pure dynamite. It's why they came for you. A sign of weakness. They're scared.'

'What's the charge?'

'There is no charge, Mia. You're on suicide watch.'

'You can't say they haven't got a sense of humour. There's nothing more frightening for the security forces than people who want to die. They can't be controlled: they're suicide killers.'

Rosentreter clears his throat; he is visibly uncomfortable.

'I've filed a suit at the High Court,' he says, tugging at his hair. 'Your proclamation hit home, but from now on we need to be really careful.'

'Tell me about my triumphs.'

Rosentreter perks up and produces a pile of newspapers from his briefcase. He holds up the first one against the Plexiglas.

'You made the front page: 10,000 CROWD DEMANDS RELEASE OF MIA HOLL.' He puts the newspaper away. 'They're standing out there with megaphones and placards. Nothing like this has happened for decades. I really wish you could hear them.'

'I *can* hear them,' says Mia.

'Listen to this,' he says, picking up another paper. 'FRAU HOLL PUTS A HOLE IN THE SYSTEM. If only the hacks were more imaginative with their puns! Here's another front-page story: METHOD UNDER ATTACK. It's written by a Herr Wörmer. He wants the Method Council to re-evaluate the Method's validity. And this one includes a letter signed by the PRI. The Alliance has come out in your support; its leadership is threatening to take action if the Method fails to admit responsibility for the death of Moritz Holl.'

'The PRI? Tell them I'm not interested. Killing innocent people isn't what I'm about.'

'You may not have a choice. From now on there are two of you. The first Mia is sitting right here and . . . her lip is bleeding.' He signals discreetly and she wipes her mouth. 'The second Mia belongs to everyone who wants her on their side.'

'Has Kramer made a statement?'

'Not really. He's supposed to be appearing on television tonight. He's been damaged badly by all this.'

'Good. He misjudged the situation.'

'Which makes him all the more dangerous.'

'Far from it. It makes him weak.'

'Mia, please, I beg you not to talk to him.'

'Who else is going to visit me?'

'You always insist on doing things your way.' Rosentreter puts away the newspapers and keeps his briefcase on his lap as if he needs something to hold on to. 'I got you all wrong.'

'Really? I thought you wanted a puppet to fight the battle for you while you wrung your hands in lawyerly despair. Well, that's exactly what you've got.'

'The flaws in my character are beyond question,' says Rosentreter. He is doing his best to hold Mia's gaze. 'The trouble is, I didn't expect things to move so quickly. I have no idea what will happen next.'

'Let me explain. Every now and then, a unifying figure comes along and people realise they're not alone with their doubts. The sceptical and the estranged, the lonely and the unhappy come together and discover the joys of community. I am the projection screen for their joy. A picture on a white wall. Full body shots. Naked, front and back. A statue of liberty, made of flesh and bone.'

As Mia straightens up and points an imaginary torch into the air, the guard in the corner lifts his chin threateningly, prompting the prisoner to sit down.

'The pheromones of togetherness can turn the lonely into a powerful force,' she says.

'Don't worry,' says Rosentreter, who has been suffering

lately from dry eyes. He blinks. 'I'll get you out of here in no time.'

'I'm not worried,' says Mia. 'If you don't get me out, the others will.'

The Healthy Mind

'Even as a young man Heinrich Kramer was committed to serving humankind.'

The voice doesn't sound like Wörmer's, although the programme is *What We All Think*. We see a man on the sofa, staring straight ahead. Dressed in a grey suit, he looks perfectly calm and unruffled – an icon of self-possession, untroubled by salivary glands, sweat ducts or bowels.

'In the wake of recent political developments we have invited him to present what is likely to be the fullest, most compelling elaboration to date of healthy thinking. Ladies and gentlemen, Heinrich Kramer!'

The man on the sofa doesn't bother with introductory remarks. Instead he takes a few seconds, staring silently at the camera, as if looking for someone beyond the lens. The notes in his hand are purely for effect. He will speak from the autocue in his head. Heinrich Kramer has devoted his life to repeating the same ideas dressed up in different words. This isn't a sign of limited imagination, but of the limited number of ideas that humans are able to draw on. There is no greater service that a man can perform for his country than repeating the right ones incessantly.

Kramer talks for twenty minutes, during which time he stares fixedly into the camera. He is making an important proclamation, as we can see from the earnestness of his expression. It would take a brave person to switch off the television and go outside. The streets are empty, like in the olden days when everyone stayed home to watch the World Cup Final. But since no one is prepared to miss Kramer's proclamation, there is no one to witness the overwhelming absence of human beings in the streets. The whole country is hanging on Kramer's words as he summarises his argument in support of the Method, each carefully worded proposition advancing with implacable logic towards the crowning point. His audience listens as he works his way through the usual line of reasoning: well-being is dependent on cleanliness and security, a lack of cleanliness is bad for the individual, inadequate security is bad for society, and faulty attitudes and faulty surveillance are responsible for disease.

The good bit comes last. Kramer talks about viruses that use uncleanliness and danger for their own ends, infecting individuals and society alike. He says the most dangerous viruses consist not of nucleic acids, but of infectious thoughts. At this point he stops. The silence continues for so long that his audience breaks into a sweat.

The Method, he says when he finally breaks the silence, is the country's immune system. And the Method has identified the latest threat. The virus is being destroyed. No one can escape the ability of a healthy body to heal itself. Santé, and goodnight.

Already the sofa is empty and Kramer has left the

studio. His exit conveys a message that everyone can read: words must be followed by deeds. The meaning of Kramer's proclamation is clear to all. It marks the beginning of the end in the case of Mia Holl.

Colourless, Odourless

It is cramped inside Mia's cell, as if the absence of furniture has shrunk the four walls. There are no chairs at the missing table. A lack of bed occupies the space beneath the window, and there isn't a wardrobe to hide the absent shelves. The whole room is replete with clinical cleanliness.

After only four days Mia is ready to welcome anyone into her cell. She needs help in occupying a space that even the furniture has abandoned. Kramer suits this purpose perfectly. A room that Kramer enters isn't empty. He brings the suggestion of furniture with him, or maybe he *is* the furniture, elegant but functional. Mia struggles to hide her excitement when he walks through the door.

'And your theories,' she says by way of a greeting, 'are as colourless and odourless as you are. They remind me of filtered water.'

'I'm glad you liked the programme – I specifically asked them to let you watch.'

'Something tells me your proclamation didn't achieve the same impact as mine.'

'Which is why I'm here – the two of us need to make some progress, take a step in the right direction.'

'The two of us?' Mia can't help laughing.

'Why not? You allowed me in here: you seem perfectly willing to talk. Besides, isn't there something glorious about the clash of our manifestos? You and I, warriors on opposing sides, visors lowered and weapons in our hands. Reason versus emotion. The rigour of my logic against the maelstrom of your feelings. The masculine versus the feminine, if you like.'

'A primitive analogy, Kramer, and beneath your intelligence. Besides, I haven't lowered my visor; I've opened it. And unless I'm much mistaken, the people are cheering me on.'

'If only they would content themselves with cheering. You've heard the news, I assume? The PRI is threatening to kill innocent people if the Method doesn't agree to your release.'

'You can't fool me that easily, Kramer. The innocent people you're so afraid for: they're cheering outside. I've got nothing to do with the PRI.'

'Society will hold you responsible if the terrorists strike.'

Mia laughs again. 'It's funny, isn't it? You want to paint me as the aggressor, and what happens? You cover me with blood. Just look at me, Kramer!'

'Gladly. The split lip is rather fetching, by the way.'

Mia leans back against the wall and spreads out her arms; clad from head to toe in white she looks like a crucified angel.

'*Your* suit is cut from the finest cloth,' she says. 'Mine is made of paper. I didn't lock myself in this cell; I didn't call for my arrest. All I did was make a pronouncement that *you* chose to publish. You've got friends in high places. They let you stroll in here, while my lawyer speaks to me through a screen. Go ahead and hold me responsible, but maybe you should ask yourself who's guiltier: the fly swatter or the fly.'

'Isn't it fascinating how Christian mythology continues to haunt our ideas? Weakness isn't the same as innocence, yet humans persist in conflating the two. David takes a swipe at Goliath, and the rabble cheers for the underdog, as if its inferiority should be prized.'

'If Goliath had some manners, he'd offer us a drink and somewhere to sit so we could have a civilised conversation. And besides, I'm hungry. Is deprivation supposed to change a person's principles?'

'I beg your pardon?' says Kramer, confused. Looking around, he seems to notice for the first time that the room is unfurnished. He pushes off from the wall and disappears through the door. Mia, eyes closed and smiling, listens to the voices in the corridor, one of which, although muffled, is diabolically piercing. A moment later Kramer returns with two folding chairs.

'I'm sorry, Frau Holl. If I were running this place, I'd dismiss those barbarians on the spot.'

'Don't apologise, Herr Kramer. They're only doing their job.'

'Sarcasm is the sign of a healthy mind; I'm glad you're bearing up. Please, take a seat.'

Gallantly he pulls up a chair for Mia and sits across from her at a suitable distance. Once seated, Mia stretches her legs, draws them in again and crosses them at the ankles. Her hands are linked behind her chair.

'You have to learn everything in here from the beginning, even how to sit. The alien sensation of brushing one's teeth with a prison toothbrush, the awkwardness of peeing while standing, the science of putting on paper overalls . . . Even language, when seldom used, is a difficult dance.'

'You dance extremely well,' says Kramer steadily. 'Now, if I could ask a few questions . . .'

'Fire away.'

'You told your lawyer that you've never felt so close to your brother.'

Mia raises her eyebrows. 'Am I to understand that you're bugging my conversations?'

'Of course. You're an enemy of the Method, hence the use of emergency powers.'

'I'm not an enemy of the Method, I'm a suicide risk.'

'It comes to the same thing.'

'Of course,' says Mia sagely.

'I was wondering how you would describe your brother's legacy − what did he leave to *you* personally?'

A guard appears at the door with a tray bearing two steaming cups and a couple of tubes of food. Kramer rises and relieves him of the tray.

'Allow me.' Respectfully he places the tubes in Mia's lap. He puts the cup of hot water on the floor and adds some lemon − three drops, just as Mia likes it. She follows his movements greedily as if the ritual of being served could satisfy a hunger more overwhelming than her physical need.

'Moritz didn't leave me any material possessions, if that's what you mean,' she says at last. 'But in spiritual terms, he gave me a lot.'

'Would you say that you're doing his will?'

Mia sips her water cautiously, puts down the cup and opens the first tube. 'All his life he did his best to bring me round to his way of thinking.'

'And he's succeeded?'

'I suppose so. Rather late in the day, you might say.'

The tube is unscrewed and Mia can't control herself any longer. Kramer watches pityingly as she squeezes its contents into her mouth.

'After his death, you went down to the river by yourself. You wanted to be close to him.'

'We started going there as kids,' says Mia through a mouthful of protein paste. 'He liked to call it our cathedral.'

'How touching.' Kramer waves a hand, allowing Mia to keep the second protein tube. 'Was anyone else involved?'

'No one.'

'Excellent, exactly as I thought! One last question. From our current perspective, Moritz is a kind of martyr, don't you think?'

'Well,' says Mia, 'it depends.'

'I beg your pardon?' Kramer leans towards her. 'I didn't quite catch that. Could you possibly speak up?'

'If it were to come to a coup,' says Mia loudly, 'Moritz would go down in history as a martyr. Which is a strange idea, by the way.'

'Marvellous.' Kramer produces a recording device from his inside pocket and switches it off. Then he sinks back in his chair, stretches his arms and checks his cuffs. 'I think that's just about everything. All I need is your signature.'

Mia stops chewing. 'My signature?'

'You need to sign your confession. You'll appreciate that the Method is very sensitive about such things.'

'My confession?'

'I meant what I said about making some progress. In your situation, it's undeniably for the best.'

'Not like that, Kramer. *I* make the rules.'

'Please, Frau Holl, there's no need to get upset. If I can summarise the main points of our conversation, perhaps you'll understand . . .' He pauses, sipping his hot water unhurriedly and gazing into his cup. Then he changes his bearing and leans into an imaginary microphone. 'Just moments ago, Method Defence confirmed that Moritz Holl has been identified as the former leader of a terrorist cell known as the Snails. The group met regularly in the woods to the south-east of the city, referred to by the Snails as the *cathedral*. Also part of the group was a certain Walter Hannemann, from whom Moritz received a bone marrow transplant and who was known to Moritz as the man who saved his life.'

Mia wrinkles her face as if she is about to burst out laughing. 'You're out of your mind!'

'Are you aware,' asks Kramer, 'that Hannemann took his life? It's tragic, really.'

'You've got his death on your conscience as well.'

'Hannemann is on your conscience, not mine.' Kramer pulls out a piece of paper and unfolds it with a torturous lack of haste. He paces around the cell, deciding where to stand. 'Are you listening, Frau Holl? It goes like this: "I, Mia Holl, worked with my brother to come up with the plan. It was simple yet ingenious. Hannemann was to murder Sibylle. As we anticipated, the crime was attributed to my brother, whose DNA was found on the deceased. The Snails regarded suicide as the apogee of personal freedom and Moritz was obsessed with the idea of martyring himself for the cause. After he was found guilty, he killed himself in prison with my help."' Kramer glances up and smiles at Mia. 'We've got it on camera. The fishing twine, you know.'

He traces a movement in the air as if he were threading something long and thin through a tiny opening. When Mia tries to leap up, he raises his hand, stopping her with a priestly gesture.

'One moment, please. I'm almost done. "The scheme was designed to provoke a legal scandal and shake the Method to its core. After Moritz's death, I took over as leader of the Snails. It was Moritz's will. The other members of the Snails are known to me only by their code names – their identities were kept secret for their own protection. My contact person was an operative known as *No one*." That's right, isn't it?' Kramer pauses. 'Incidentally, *No one* is a code name for a younger colleague of mine, Herr Wörmer from *What We All Think*. Most regrettable.'

Mia is on her feet. She rushes at Kramer, but he leaps up and catches her fists. For a few seconds they wrestle in silence, then Mia surrenders and slumps against him. It is almost like a lovers' embrace.

'Sometimes you realise that the smell of another human being is a wonderful thing,' she says softly.

'You're a good girl.' Kramer strokes her hair gently. 'A brave girl. A lonely girl.'

At that, Mia pushes him away with both hands and tugs wildly at her overalls. She smooths her hair. 'You'll never get away with it.'

Kramer shakes his head slightly as he reaches into his trouser pocket and pulls out a plastic bag, which he proceeds to pull over his right hand.

'I wouldn't be so sure,' he says. 'Haven't you ever wondered why Moritz was on a blind date with a woman who was murdered by his stem cell donor that very night?'

'There's such a thing as coincidence.'

'Even for scientists?'

'You know very well that it wasn't a terrorist plot.'

'Really? It fits together beautifully, don't you think? Very convincing.' Smiling, Kramer transfers the empty protein tubes to his plastic bag, carefully avoiding any contact with his skin. 'Let the poison of doubt do its work. At least you'll have something to think about in your spare time.'

'You're beasts!' shrieks Mia. 'You're cold-blooded murderers!' She points in what she thinks is the direction of the prison's main door. 'I'll tell the people outside about your criminal system; they'll smash down the doors!'

'The people outside,' says Kramer, pointing politely in the opposite direction, 'will believe what they want to believe. So you're determined not to sign, Frau Holl?'

'I expected better of you, Kramer — more sophistication, fewer outright lies. It's humiliating to be hitched to such a rickety wagon. You really *don't* have a conscience at all.'

Kramer has placed the plastic package of tubes into

his bag. He turns to look at Mia and smiles: his face shows no trace of satisfaction or scorn.

'Why don't we call it a sense of honour? Not so long ago you accused me of thinking that all political systems were essentially the same. Let's assume you were right. Let's also assume that we agree on this point. Whatever the system, everywhere in the world you see unhappy, unsmiling faces. In our system, there's a respectable proportion of smiles. Isn't that enough, Frau Holl?'

'Moritz had to die for a smile?' says Mia through gritted teeth. 'Moritz and Hannemann – and whoever you've lined up next.'

Kramer ignores her objections. 'Anyone with a talent for analytical thinking must resign himself to living in a vacuum – or choose a path. You made a choice, Frau Holl, but decisions are only real when you're faced with their consequences. The consequences take hold of you, and they don't let you go. The biggest danger is opportunism and the only defence is a sense of honour. I'm bound to my cause by my sense of honour and the same is true for you.'

'Are you trying to convince me *not* to put my signature to your pack of lies?'

'Maybe, my sweet,' says Kramer, smiling slightly. 'But I'll come back and ask you again to sign. Santé.'

Wörmer

Judge Hutschneider is a man of some sixty years with a full beard and most of his professional life behind him. His children speak four languages; his son lives in Paris, his daughter in New York. At weekends he takes the Cityhopper to visit his grandchildren, whose faces are pasted inside a locket around his wife's neck. The outside of the locket bears the family crest, likewise the mat outside the front door. When the Hutschneiders refer to their house as their 'abode', they do so without a hint of irony. Judge Hutschneider's life is an immaculate chain of correct decisions: the doormat, the locket, Paris and New York. He leads an orderly, peaceful existence in which there is no place whatsoever for the Mia Holl affair.

Now that Sophie has been stood down from the trial and transferred to a provincial court, Hutschneider has been dragged out of semi-retirement and installed as her replacement. The boost to his pension does little to console him: Mia Holl is not a defendant; she is a time bomb. Since his appointment as presiding judge, his house has been besieged by journalists, none of whom pay any attention to the crest on the mat. The crowds outside the law courts are slowly thinning, but Hutschneider is still obliged to sneak round the back. And his office has been colonised by Method Defence.

Hutschneider has never had such reason to be grateful that his children live abroad. Humans are very vulnerable, even when their every movement is supervised by two inscrutable bodyguards with transmitters in their ears. Humans breathe, eat and drink – they touch things with *bare hands*. And a rumour has been circulating that the Snails are about to launch a large-scale chemical attack. Under the circumstances Hutschneider is reluctant to play the hero, especially when the well-being of his family is at stake. One false move could ruin his chances of a peaceful retirement, and Hutschneider, by his own admission, is no match for Mia Holl. Luckily, there are people who are trained to deal with terrorists, and he has taken their advice.

Despite the experts' warnings not to get emotionally involved, Hutschneider is immediately affected by the sight of the defendant, seated mere metres away behind a Plexiglas screen. With her slight frame and hollow face, against which her eyes are unnaturally big and bright, she doesn't look like a potential mass murderer. He thinks of clever, discerning Sophie, who was duped by this woman, and reminds himself that no one can see into another person's soul. And with all respect to human nature, he isn't much tempted to try.

Contrary to his usual practice, Hutschneider has brought a complete edition of the Method's statutes to the hearing. The volumes are lined up like a barricade across his desk.

'Frau Holl,' he says, 'I'd like you to tuck your hair

behind your ears and raise your head properly. Look towards me . . . Thank you, that's right.'

Mia complies. She is sitting on a stool, with a straight back and something resembling pride. She looks at the judge with torturous determination. Her gaze conveys a mixture of childish outrage, anguished hope and utter dismay. For the first time in his life Hutschneider wishes he were wearing dark glasses.

'Please summon the chief witness,' he says to the microphone on his desk.

Barely a second later, the door opens and a pair of guards bring in a man in handcuffs. Like Mia, he is wearing overalls made of white paper. The lower half of his face is obscured by a hygiene mask. Hutschneider gestures for the guards to lead him to the Plexiglas partition.

'*No one*,' he says, 'do you recognise this woman?'

The chief witness doesn't hesitate. 'Her name is Mia Holl.' He scans the courtroom nervously, not looking at the defendant.

'Good gracious,' says Mia, staring pityingly at the handcuffed man. 'What on earth did they do to you?'

Hutschneider activates his digital recorder. 'Point one. Let it be noted that the defendant, on seeing the chief witness, greeted him in the manner of a friend,' he says.

'Is Kramer making you do this?' asks Mia.

'She's Moritz Holl's sister,' says *No one* in the flat tone of a person reading from a script.

'You're Wörmer, aren't you? The TV presenter. "Legitimate governments are like custom-made shoes – they never pinch or rub." That was you, wasn't it? I thought it was good.'

'Point two. Let it be noted that the defendant has identified the witness by name. She shares his views.'

'Mia Holl replaced her brother Moritz as the leader of the Snails,' continues Wörmer.

'You don't have to say that,' says Mia sadly.

'I was her contact person. I used to meet her in the cathedral.'

'Point three. The chief witness has identified the defendant as the leader of an anti-Method faction.'

No one turns to face the judge. 'That's all,' he says.

'Wörmer,' says Mia, 'when you wrote your article, you must have been thinking about me, an innocent citizen at the mercy of the Method.'

'Can I go?' asks *No one*. 'Right now.'

'And while you were writing the article, you must have imagined what it would be like to talk to me, to tell me your thoughts, to express the things you'd never said. You must have imagined how good it would be to talk to someone and look them in the eye.'

'Point four. The defendant addressed the chief witness and made reference to their shared beliefs.'

No one glances around frantically and tries to beckon the guards with his manacled hands. 'I've made my statement,' he says.

'I'm right here, Wörmer. You can see my eyes. You can hear my voice. Lean against the Plexiglas and you'll smell me as well.'

'Point five. The chief witness concluded his statement and left the stand,' says Hutschneider to his digital recorder.

'Look at me,' says Mia, raising her voice. 'I stand for

what we all think! I'm the *corpus delicti*. Look me in the eye and repeat your lies.'

'Take him away,' says Hutschneider.

No one casts a quick look at Mia; the guards tug him away and march him out of the room. The judge hurries to gather up his books.

'Since life,' says Mia, 'is meaningless and yet you have to keep going, I sometimes feel like making sculptures out of copper pipes. I could weld them together and make a crane, or pile them up randomly like a nest of fossilised *worms*. A good joke, wouldn't you say, Judge Hutschneider? Why aren't you laughing?'

Mia laughs. She is still laughing as Hutschneider closes his briefcase. She is laughing, thinks Hutschneider, at *him*. He leaves the courtroom in haste.

No Love in the World

He is a terrible actor. He knows that she knows that he knows − and so on and so forth until the end of time. Rosentreter is on his way to the visitors' room and already he feels exposed. Ever since Moritz was proven innocent, there has been a strange look in Mia's eyes. It seems to pass through everything, as if the world were made of glass. It is a look that hurts, a look that is best avoided, especially by people bearing bad news. And Rosentreter's head, hands, shirt pockets and trouser pockets are spilling over with bad news. In fact, he is ready to believe that he himself is a piece of bad news. The upbeat expression he assumes as he walks through the door puts a strain on his cheeks. He isn't surprised to see that Mia is there already. He can't recall a single occasion when he has arrived in time to see her walk through the door: she is always there before him, standing or sitting as the situation demands. It is almost as if she has been left there, in exactly the right location to deliver her lines. Rosentreter imagines a zip running down her back and cables in her belly. Over the past few days he has caught himself starting to hate her. He is ashamed of himself for hating her and ashamed that it makes him feel better. It simplifies the situation. It is a relief to hate Mia, to hate her without the slightest justification and with all his heart.

She looks in his direction and waits motionless as he takes up position on the other side of the Plexiglas. Her face is drawn and Rosentreter wonders if they are giving her enough to eat. If he is honest with himself, he doesn't really want to know. Given the choice, he would like the matter to be over. Since his historic victory in the courtroom, things have taken a wrong turn. Mia is to blame. *She* was the one who refused to follow his advice; *she* was the one who insisted on her radical stance. She opened the door to the predatory Kramer – and why? In Rosentreter's eyes, there can only be one explanation: Mia is obsessive, masochistic and, very likely, psychologically disturbed. Things had started so well: he had taken the initiative and triumphed in court. Then Mia hijacked the situation and insisted on pursuing her own crazy goals. Rosentreter can't do much to help her at this stage. Legally, this is known as superseding causation. It is a simple question of accountability. Mia wanted to be the cause of something, thus Mia alone is responsible for the consequences. There isn't the slightest reason for her lawyer to feel bad on her behalf.

Mia's face brightens as soon as Rosentreter takes a seat. 'Hello,' she says simply.

She is clearly pleased to see him, which makes Rosentreter hate her more. He privately attributes his emotional state to confusion. He feels thoroughly out of his depth. He doesn't know how to start the conversation, much less where to take it from there. Mia comes to his aid.

'It's quite simple,' she says, while Rosentreter wonders, not without anxiety, whether she can read his thoughts. 'You draw air into your lungs, you raise your soft palate, air passes over your vocal cords, and you move your lips and tongue. Or, to put it another way, you speak.'

She smiles. She was probably trying to be funny. At this point she places her hand on the partition in a comforting gesture, whereupon Rosentreter is stricken with such despair that he finally finds the impetus to pull himself together.

'The High Court has dismissed your, I mean, *our* appeal.' He clears his throat. 'The judge cited insufficient prospect of success.'

'So I'm stuck here?'

'Apparently so. The application for exemption was rejected as well. You'll have to go back to court.'

'We were expecting as much, were we not?'

'Yes.'

'Did you bring the papers? Tell me what they're saying.'

'Are you sure you want to know?'

'I insist.'

Rosentreter produces a small stack of daily papers. It includes only the least condemnatory articles.

'*New Information in the Case of Mia Holl,*' he reads out. '*Detectives Uncover Botulinum Stash.*'

'Botulinum?' asks Mia.

'Should I carry on reading?'

'Of course! What's the matter with you?'

'Maybe I should tell you myself.' Rosentreter puts down the papers and gets out a tissue to wipe his palms.

'Bacterial cultures were found in your apartment. In protein tubes, to be precise.'

'In my apartment?' Mia thinks for a second; her face clouds over. 'Of course . . . That's why Kramer needed those things!'

'Your fingerprints were found on the tubes. Inside were fifty grams of botulinum.'

'Fifty grams is enough to wipe out half the population.'

'Someone in your laboratory is quoted as saying you worked with botulinum.'

'That was a decade ago – a pharmacological research project.'

'Irrelevant, Mia. Method Defence has sifted your data: telephone calls, conversations in your apartment, electronic messages.'

'And?'

'Drawings of the city's water supply were found on your computer.'

'I live in a monitored house. I've got drawings of the electricity supply and the drains as well.'

'An outbreak of botulism would be catastrophic.'

'You do realise this is utter nonsense?'

'Yes.'

'So what do we do?'

'I complained about them searching your apartment, but they were careful. Not the slightest breach of protocol. Legal warrant, approval of the judge. The discovery of the botulinum was witnessed by two independent observers. A Frau Poll and a Lizzie someone-or-other.'

'I bet they were pleased.'

'It's isn't easy to pick holes in Method Defence's investigations. Impossible, some might say.'

Mia nods slowly, wrapped up in her thoughts. At last she cocks her head as if listening to something. 'They've stopped calling for my release, haven't they?'

'Yes,' says Rosentreter regretfully. 'They've all gone.'

'It's funny. I can hear them.'

'And rightly so!' Rosentreter brings his palm down against the plastic arm of the chair. 'We're not giving in! I'll appeal again to the High Court. I'll petition the Method Council and explain our stance. There's a young journalist I can . . .'

Mia lifts her head. 'Do you want to resign from the case?'

'Resign?' says Rosentreter. 'I didn't say anything about resigning!'

'I wouldn't blame you if you did. If you want to quit, tell me now.'

For a short moment neither says anything as they follow their thoughts. Then Rosentreter flexes his spine and packs the newspapers into his case. Of course he would rather withdraw from the case. In an ideal world, he would never set eyes on Mia Holl again. But precisely because she made the suggestion, he finds himself unable to act. Some people, he thinks, aren't made to be heroes or criminals: the majority of us, in fact.

When he replies, he surprises himself by sounding very determined. 'No,' he says. 'We're going to fight this together.'

'If you're sure.'

Mia doesn't look especially pleased by his decision to

stay on the case. Maybe, thinks Rosentreter, she has long since stopped caring whether or not anyone is acting in her defence. She may have understood the truth of the situation; perhaps more clearly than him. In fact, her understanding of her future might be like her personality: cool, meticulous, without sentiment. In which case she is bound to know that appeals and petitions aren't relevant now. It isn't about the botulinum; it's about the fact that a person's data trail can be taken apart and reassembled in a million different ways. If the Method thinks Mia Holl is a threat to the system, the Method will perceive her as a threat. Rosentreter has only to look at Mia from an angle so that her nose protrudes sharply from her profile and her eyes look particularly deep-set, and he sees it too. At least until she smooths her hair with both hands and smiles at him.

'Anyway,' she says chattily. 'How are things with you?'

'Well,' says Rosentreter, who for days now has been asking himself the same question without reaching a conclusion, 'I've . . . I've split up with my, um, friend.'

'What do you mean?' For the first time Mia looks upset. 'You can't have done! A woman like cold water on burnt skin . . .'

'It was for the best. We couldn't stop arguing. We've been arguing for weeks. About you.'

'She didn't think we were . . . ?'

'No.' The lawyer smiles bitterly. 'If only she had. It would have made things easier. She couldn't understand why I would put myself in danger by taking on your case. She accused me of hard-nosed careerism. In the end I had to level with her. I told her I was tired of feeling like a fugitive because I'd met the woman of my dreams. I told her I wanted to send a clear signal; that I had to do something when the opportunity arose.' Rosentreter puts his hands to his face; his voice sounds empty. 'When she finally understood, she went mad. She's a gentle person, really; she'd never shouted at me like that before. She wanted to know why I thought our feelings were more important than the Method. She said no love in the world could justify defending a terrorist.'

'A terrorist?'

'I had to let it go, don't you see? I couldn't tell her the truth. She lives a normal life. She's like other normal people; she doesn't believe in anything – except what she reads in the papers. I couldn't destroy her world; it wouldn't be right.'

'To lose your destination and your point of departure is a cruel twist of fate,' says Mia. 'A perfidious metaphor of meaninglessness. I don't envy you.'

Rosentreter lowers his hands and looks at Mia with reddened eyes. 'You think your situation is better?'

'Of course. I can always tell myself that Moritz would have wanted this – and this, and this, and this . . . Yes, he would have wanted this. That's where I've got the upper hand: he isn't here to argue.'

Rosentreter stands up hastily and collects his things. Everyone has a pain threshold; Mia has pushed him over his.

'I'm sorry,' he says. 'I have to go.

'Come closer to the screen,' whispers Mia.

They place their hands against the glass.

'Did you bring it? It's the only favour I've ever asked.'

He drops his left hand into his jacket pocket and hides something between his fingers. He leans towards the screen and feeds something through the constellation of circular holes while pretending to kiss the glass.

'Thank you.' Mia closes her fingers around the object. This time it isn't fishing twine; it's a long needle.

The Middle Ages

'I'll set the record straight!' Mia looks at Kramer and turns away; her gaze runs scared. 'Botulinum in protein tubes! Don't make me laugh. You and I are going to tighten up the science in your terrorist plot. I'll tell my side of the story, and you'll be my mouthpiece. Do you have a pen?'

'Mia, this isn't the right moment for another public statement. The situation is under control. You and I are going to sit tight and wait for the weekend revolutionaries to see the error of their ways and scuttle home.'

'Do as you like, but I'm not keeping quiet. I want to speak to my supporters.'

'I'm sorry, Mia.'

'I told you to get your pen!' She attacks with raised claws, aiming for his face, as she did in the confrontation with Method Defence. There is nothing to which humans beings become accustomed more quickly than violence.

'I've stopped caring!' she shouts wildly. 'That makes me dangerous!'

'It makes you *embarrassing*,' says Kramer, not attempting to defend himself.

Mia runs aground on his passivity; she drops her arms. It might be easy to fight back, scratching and kicking, against a superior assailant. It takes an expert, though, to attack a man leaning casually against the wall with his hands in his pockets.

'OK,' says Kramer, which isn't a word he often uses. If Mia knew him better, she would realise that he is still in shock from her attack. But Mia's strength has gone.

'Let's get down to business.' Kramer shakes the events of the last few moments from his jacket sleeves. He paces up and down as if he were delivering a lecture. 'In one of our earlier conversations, we touched on the function of the defendant's confession in criminal law. If a confession is not forthcoming, the subjective truth of the defendant must be replaced with an approximation of objective truth: in other words, we construct a perfect chain of proof — witness statements, fingerprints, voice recordings and so forth.'

'DNA tests are popular,' says Mia in a whisper.

Kramer pretends not to hear. 'In your case, the chain of evidence is complete. All the same, the Method is keen to elicit a confession. You're being offered certain privileges.'

'Privileges?' Mia lifts her head; she seems confused. She looks Kramer in the eye and a moment later she understands what the substance of the negotiations is to be. A state based on the Method, a state that takes human existence as its highest principle, cannot sentence its citizens to death. Instead, the ultimate penalty is *vita minima*, virtual death, which comes with the promise of rehabilitation, should the political circumstances change. It's a sensible solution, though unpleasant for those concerned. If you die, you get away, Moritz used to say. But if you're frozen, you belong to the system for good. You're their trophy.

'So you're prepared to go all the way,' says Mia, breaking the silence. 'I don't even know what I'm charged with.'

'Of course you do, Mia. They used to call it high treason.'

'What do they call it now?'

'Method Defence has intervened on your behalf. Barker and Hutschneider are willing to commute your sentence in return for a confession. You'll get a prison sentence instead of freezing. With a bit of luck, they'll move you to a more comfortable facility once you've served a few years. You're still young.'

'Do you think I'm going to confess to your ridiculous botulinum plot? I'm not going to stand up in court and say that my brother's death was the work of some fictional terrorist cell. You're insane!'

'If I were you, I'd think about it carefully.'

'There's no need. Everything I ever cared about has been taken from me: Moritz, my apartment, my work, my belief in something approximating justice, as far as it went. Do you know what I'm left with?'

'No – but I'm bracing myself for another of your twentieth-century anachronisms.'

'I'm left with my soul,' says Mia. 'My honour, my dignity . . . If it amuses you to freeze me, go right ahead.'

'You can be certain that Moritz wouldn't have wanted *that*.'

'How dare you!' screams Mia. 'I hope you choke on his name if you ever mention it again!'

'Good gracious,' says Kramer in mock terror, tracing a

crucifix in the air. 'A witch's curse. *Vade retro!* I'm sorry, Mia, it isn't a laughing matter, of course. The whole episode with Moritz was a tremendous setback. For the first time, the Method showed itself to be fallible. You realise we've had terrorist threats.'

'I thought the weekend revolutionaries had gone home.'

'The PRI has gained momentum. Quite apart from that, compliance with health and hygiene regulations has fallen. Do you understand how serious that is?' He leans forward as if there were nothing more natural than to reach for her hand. He seems to think they have been wedded by circumstances. 'If society doesn't work together to maintain security and hygiene, we'll be hit by an epidemic in a matter of weeks. These days, we're immunologically vulnerable.'

'What has this got to do with me?'

'From now on your brother's name will be invoked to justify every subversive act in the country. History teaches us that isolated events can lead to appalling bloodshed – the defenestrations of Prague, the storming of the Bastille, the Archduke's murder in Sarajevo, the death of Moritz Holl. Be reasonable, Mia! You say you've found your true self. Do you think you should burden it with such responsibility?'

'Burden?' Mia shrugs her shoulders. 'It doesn't feel like a burden to me.'

Kramer takes another step towards her. 'If you had it in your power to stop the Archduke being murdered, would you?'

'Maybe,' says Mia hesitantly.

'That's the problem, Mia. Past actions can't be retracted, but the future can be changed. Millions of people depend on the Method. Are you going to risk their lives for the sake of your dignity? Is it honourable to value your self above all else? What should we value most, Mia? What is humankind compared to your dignity?'

'How should I know?' says Mia defiantly.

'I recommend you think about it. I'm giving you twenty-four hours.'

'You're wasting your time. I won't betray my brother or myself.'

'That's your final word?'

'It's pretty straightforward. You think you can change my mind because I haven't argued rationally. You're wrong. I don't need rational arguments: the fewer I use, the stronger I become.'

'Mia . . .' Kramer rubs his hands together, slips them into his pockets, takes them out. For a moment he almost resembles Rosentreter. He is obviously wrestling with an uncomfortable piece of news. 'Mia, the Method is making you an offer. It has other ways of asking, if you know what I mean.'

When Mia says nothing, Kramer resumes pacing up and down the cell. 'Mia, this conversation isn't over. I'm sure you're aware that the Method's handling of criminal justice is extremely progressive, but progress is never an entirely straight line. In certain situations, in highly sensitive cases, when there is a threat to the greater good, a degree of backsliding has been known to occur. In such situations, the system may revert to somewhat *medieval* methods . . .'

For a few seconds, Mia stares at him, appalled. 'Tell me straight,' she says when she is finally able to speak. 'What are they going to do to me?'

'The basic procedure is nothing new. The same methods were used half a century ago. They'll stand you on a crate, naked, of course, and place a black hood over your head. Contacts will be attached to your fingers, toes and genitalia – like clothes pegs.' He presses his thumb against his forefinger as if he were opening and closing a peg. 'They'll start with maximum current – no messing about with incremental shocks. Two senior clinicians from the university hospital will be present to make sure you don't . . . how should I put it? . . . pass away.'

Mia shakes her head, hiccups with laughter, turns away and runs to the door. It is locked. She rattles the handle vigorously, then she stops and raises a hand, tracing a finger over the cold metal as if checking the smoothness of the surface.

'So there we have it: the system may revert to medieval methods.' She turns round, laughing. 'But deep down we knew as much, didn't we, Kramer? You more than anyone. But I knew as well. Nothing has changed. Nothing ever changes. One system is as good as another. The Middle Ages is not a historical period; the Middle Ages is the name of human nature.'

'Harsh words, but not entirely unjustified. So you're not going to change your mind?'

'No. Will you be there to watch?'

'Not if I can help it.' Kramer clears his throat. 'I'm rather squeamish, but if you insist . . .'

'*It*' is Raining

'It's only my body. A body. Only the body.'

It is clear from Mia's voice that she has been talking to herself for many hours.

'My toes belong to my body. My fingers belong to my body. My genitalia belong to my body. My arms and legs belong to my body. My stomach belongs to my body. My heart belongs to my body. My brain . . .' She stops for a moment; a spasm takes hold of her shoulders and her head bangs up and down against the floor. 'My brain belongs to my body. A world of matter staring at itself. They can have it! Moritz would be pleased.'

Another spasm takes hold of her and she tries to slot a hand beneath her right temple to cushion her skull. She is shaking as if she were still attached to the machine. Some time ago, they removed the crate and cables and left Mia on the floor. Curled up like an embryo, she is alone in her cell. She hasn't moved from the spot, save for the spasms. The floor is tiled, which makes it hard and cold. In a sense, she is lucky to have lost sensation in her body. The bigger problem, from her perspective, is the flickering light. Every 1.5 seconds the light turns off and on. Mia's body is bathed in blinding light and plunged into darkness again, and again. A constant flickering, off, on. A free man is like a faulty bulb. That's how Moritz put it.

The light stops her sleeping. It interrupts her thoughts. Each new flash of light cuts into her brain like a knife. There is no rest. No loss of consciousness. No sinking into merciful oblivion. They have condemned Mia, or what is left of Mia, to being wide awake.

'The good thing about a sister, you once said to me, is not having to *believe* in her. According to you, that's what distinguished me, your sister, from God, from you, and from everything you said and did. I said no one except God was stupid enough to need constant proof of his own existence. You looked at me seriously and said God's existence was long proven. You gave me three proofs of his existence: there is no God, God is a figment of your imagination, and God is dead. I made you explain. No one, you said, comments on a thing that doesn't exist; no one points out its non-existence or claims that it's dead. Otherwise, you said, the world would be full of statements like "Casmanets are a figment of your imagination!" or "Teezle is dead". What, I asked, are casmanets? And who is Teezle? You laughed and laughed. See, you said, they don't exist! It's a good thing we're not obliged to point out the non-existence of the non-existent in order to stop it from existing; it would take all day, you said. I think you were twelve at the time.'

When the next spasm comes she manages to hold both hands beneath her head and roll a little to the side. She is almost on her back.

'Of course, I laughed too. Laughing was wonderful;

laughing together was fun, especially when we were kids and you were discovering philosophy. Philosophy was laughter that never seemed to stop. You said that nothing was a given, especially the world. Who gave it? The same impersonal *it* that rains? The same *it* that is high time? The same *it* that is possible, impossible, obvious and clear? If so, God and *I* have a lot in common. They're nothing but pronouns. A grammatical bind.'

A noise escapes from Mia: with a bit of imagination, we could construe it as a laugh or a cough.

'You were so smart. After that I couldn't say "it's raining" without smiling to myself. Maybe it's raining now . . . What season is it? We should all have a tree outside our window or a steep slate roof on the other side of the street, something to tell us if it's raining. Darkness should be a human right. Maybe I'll start a campaign. The point of night is to adjust ourselves gradually to darkness. The point of sleep is to adjust ourselves to death, night after night. Turn off the light. Sometimes a long train of thought leads nowhere but autumn.'

For a while Mia lies in silence, tapping her foot limply in time with the rhythm of the light until her head is full again, her mind overrun by the ceaseless, intrusive and unnecessary production of thoughts. An impenetrable jungle of musings. Speech is a scythe.

'Your knees are my only chair. Your back is my table. Your eyes are my windows. May your mouth be the glass from which I drink, your heart my sustenance, your pulse my watch, your life my time. May your breath be my air. May your face be my moon when you bend over me at night, and my sun when you laugh for me in the light.

May your voice be my only sound, your pulse be my watch, your life be my time. May your death be mine.'

The spasms return with a vengeance, causing Mia to throw her head from side to side as if her thoughts were pestering her like flies. When her temple hits the floor again, pain oozes into her, seeping through her right ear, spreading like acid through her lower jaw, numbing her lips, closing her right eye. Mia sees her head as an ants' nest made entirely of delicate walkways filled with poison. Then darkness comes at last.

Thin Air

She hears the sound of falling water, an irregular bright patter, too loud for rain. It smells of vinegar. When Mia opens her eyes, she is looking straight into Kramer's face. It doesn't strike her as unusual: she has long felt that his image is inscribed on the inside of her eyelids.

'What are you doing?' she asks.

'Working on your resurrection.' He dips a sponge into a bowl and draws it across her brow. 'How are you feeling?'

'Terrific. I'll soon be well enough to dash your brains out.'

'That's wonderful news,' says Kramer.

Without warning Mia's head moves in a spasm, jerking to the side and knocking the bowl from Kramer's hand.

'Sorry,' she says. 'Collateral damage — although I don't suppose anyone is counting any more.'

'That's what I'm here to discuss.'

Kramer has brought two chairs. During his last visit, he and Mia sat on these chairs and chatted. She hasn't seen them since.

This time, Kramer has to scoop Mia into his arms and

place her on the chair. Her body must be rearranged carefully to ensure she is balanced.

'During the witch hunts,' says Mia, 'if a person survived being tortured, they let her go.'

'I'm afraid the excursion to the Middle Ages is over.'

Mia looks at Kramer and jerks her chin towards a corner of the cell. 'Over there.'

Kramer hovers, uncertain as to whether to sit down. 'I'm sorry?'

'Just do it, won't you?'

He turns and follows her directions. 'Do you know the craziest thing about all this?' he says.

'Kneel.'

Kramer looks at Mia, who is balanced helplessly on the chair; then he drops to his knees and continues to talk. He looks old-fashioned, like a Christian at prayer.

'It didn't occur to me until yesterday,' he says, 'and I haven't stopped thinking about it since. It seemed to me that I'd dealt with life's key questions in my youth. I'd always assumed that a well-regulated human life consisted of four main stages. The first twenty years are spent thinking. In the next twenty, you speak; in the third stage, you act; and in the final stage, you return to thinking. I recently made the transition from speaking to acting.'

'Put your hand on the tiles and run your finger along the gap,' says Mia.

Kramer does as he is bidden and slots a finger between the tiles. 'Then you came along. Suddenly I'm back in a thinking phase again.'

He sounds in a good mood. Still on his knees, he raises his head to look at Mia as if expecting her to rejoice in his intellectual rejuvenation. But Mia's attention is focused on something closer to hand. Summoning all her remaining strength, she sits straight in her chair and screws up her eyes, straining to see.

'Have you found it?'

Kramer gets up, holding a long needle between his thumb and index finger. 'Do you mean this?'

'Well done,' says Mia. 'Now come over here.'

Kramer stands in front of her obediently. 'Don't you want to know what I'm thinking about?'

Mia takes the needle from him and shakes her head – this time, intentionally.

'You accused me of fanaticism,' says Kramer. 'But you're the one who wants to die for your freshly minted beliefs. Doesn't that strike you as odd?'

'Bend down.'

Kramer bends at the hips and places his hands on his knees like a goalkeeper. His face is level with hers. As they look at each other in close-up, Mia raises the needle and points it at his right eye.

'The question is,' he says, 'how can you tell the martyr from the fanatic? I chose my side decades ago and I've sacrificed everything. I'll continue to sacrifice everything, including the most valuable human possession: my time on this Earth. Meanwhile, you chose your side yesterday and you're intent on sacrificing your life in a struggle you're going to lose. Surely that makes me the martyr and you the fanatic?'

Mia holds the needle millimetres from his eye. 'Aren't you scared?'

'No,' he says.

'That's the difference,' says Mia. '*I* am. My fanaticism is a weaker, paler version of yours.' She lowers the needle. 'Can you believe I went to the trouble of getting this needle because I wanted to jab you in the eye and pierce your brain. That's how much you mattered. I'm wiser now: the sharpest weapons should be directed against the self.'

Kramer doesn't try to stop her. A few seconds ago, he watched while she threatened him with a needle, now he watches while she prepares to harm herself. Wrinkling his nose in disgust, he steps back as she rolls up her left sleeve, pats her upper arm and raises her right hand. The speed of entry isn't curbed by doubt. The needle buries itself in Mia's arm, deep below the skin.

'Which of us,' asks Kramer, turning away, 'is the criminal now?'

'If you're starting to doubt yourself,' says Mia through gritted teeth, 'don't worry. I assure you: no one is more despicable than you.'

Blood is coursing down her arm, forming crimson pools on her paper suit. Twisting her head as far as possible to get a better view, Mia grips the needle firmly and drags it in circles to open the wound.

'This here,' she says, 'is your work. You are the needle, the arm, the blood. You are the rightful owner of the sorry remains of what used to be a contented woman — whatever that means. You should listen to yourself, Heinrich Kramer. First you destroy me; then you accuse me of having nothing to lose. I like a man with a sense of humour!' Her head shakes uncontrollably as she is seized by a spasm. 'See how you value your superior reasoning, your analytical distance! You pride yourself on not being a fanatic, but do you know the truth? You're worse than a fanatic: you're a fanatic embarrassed by your fanaticism. Shall I tell you what makes that especially repellent?'

'By all means. But have pity on me, Mia. You're making me nauseous with all that digging into your flesh.'

But Mia has no intention of halting her investigation into the bleeding wound.

'A fanatic,' she says, 'is someone who clings to his ideas like a child to his mother's skirt. He wants to be mummy's darling; only then will he be happy and fulfilled. But that's not enough for Heinrich Kramer. He wants to be mummy's darling *and* he wants to despise her.' She laughs. 'You style yourself as a free thinker and a martyr, but it all comes down to a conceptual sleight of hand.'

'Mummy's darling . . . A telling analogy, don't you think?'

'Only with regard to *you*. Your mother is the Method and you're shuddering with desire for the prime position at her breast. Maybe my last task on Earth is to teach you what it means to be an adult. Watch carefully – ah, here it is!'

Mia is crouched over her arm. She digs her fingernails into the wound.

'You're talking like a bad loser,' says Kramer. He sounds less sure of himself than usual.

'Winner? Loser? You're wasting your time! Who do you think is going to judge us? We've climbed too high, the storms are below us, the air is too thin. We can scream, but we won't get an answer; we won't even hear an echo.

You want to know if you're a fanatic or a martyr? No one is going to tell you. You're asking questions of the void! You want to cast yourself as a good person in spite of everything; a better person than me? Go right ahead. The universe doesn't care. And neither do I.'

'This isn't a moral dilemma; I merely wanted to know—'

'Look, Kramer, a present for you.' Mia holds out her hand and offers him the bloody microchip from her arm. 'Take it. It's me. It is rightfully yours. Turn it into a pendant or something.'

'Thank you,' says Kramer, taking out a white handkerchief and picking up the chip.

'The rest of me stays here and belongs to no one, therefore to everyone.' Mia allows herself to slide sideways off the chair to the floor. 'Completely vulnerable; completely free. A sacred state. You can go now. The rest of me wants to sleep.'

Kramer starts to say something and stops when he realises her eyes are already closed. For a few seconds he gazes at her peaceful face, then he shrugs.

'The false pride of the martyr,' he says. But even he doesn't seem to trust the scorn in his voice.

See Above

'Forgive me, Mia. I'm so sorry.'

Everyone is there. In Mia's blurred vision, the court-room stretches to infinity, the rows of spectators filling her view. She looks in vain among the black-robed manne-quins for the woman with the blonde ponytail. Instead she sees that the middle chair has been claimed by a grey-bearded judge. She recognises him from last time, and she didn't know how to get through to him then.

Mia is so distracted by the commotion that she barely pays attention to the hands that a moment ago were gripping the bars of her cage, or to the voice begging forgiveness over and over again. We can assume that the hands and voice belonged to Rosentreter, who has vanished from Mia's view. Perhaps they have dragged him away. Mia finds it not unpleasant being locked in a cage. She is a theatregoer, watching the spectacle from a private box. The only irritation is the hissing of the atomisers, one in each corner of the cage, releasing clouds of disinfectant. The pauses between squirts are like the moments of darkness in the flick-ering light of the cell where Mia suspects she lost her mind. Everything she can see and hear seems to have

sprung from a crazed imagination. The black mannequins are presiding over crowds of shouting and
chanting people. From what Mia can make out, they
are calling for her head, although she can't see the use
of a head without its contents. At the front of the room,
the bearded judge, who looks even more miserable than
usual, bangs his gavel.

At last it is still. A doctor in a white coat approaches
the cage. Mia shrinks away from him, as if he were
intending to put electrical contacts on her fingers and
toes. The guards push her into a corner with their sticks.
The doctor reaches an arm through the bars and scans
Mia's bicep. Everyone's gaze is fixed on the projection
wall, which shows an empty rectangle of light. Mia
laughs. The atomiser hisses. The scanner emits a piercing
beep. The doctor notices the scab on Mia's arm and hurries
to the front of the room to whisper something to the
presiding judge, who nods.

'The court is ready,' says Hutschneider. 'The Method
versus Mia Holl.'

A black mannequin rises and turns his face towards
Mia. It is Prosecutor Barker. As he reads out a practically
endless list of charges, Mia slowly begins to grasp what
is going on.

'Orchestrating a terrorist campaign,' says Barker.
'Conspiring to murder Sibylle Meiler. Attempting to cause
civil unrest. Defying the orders of armed officials.'

Each of the leading players is given a last chance to
take to the stage like actors giving a final curtain call. It
is fitting, thinks Mia. A nice idea.

'Anti-Method activities. Subverting the Method and its

administrative organs. Consorting with persons hostile to the Method. Using violence against representatives of the Method. Inciting civil disobedience. Disturbing the peace.'

Mia raises her arms, preparing to applaud.

'Conspiring to contaminate the drinking supply. High treason. Leadership of a terrorist organisation. The prosecution demands the maximum sentence: freezing of the defendant for an unlimited term.'

When Barker falls silent, Mia is the only one to applaud.

A member of the public leaps to his feet. 'Stop the witch hunt!' he shouts. 'No more show trials!'

His neighbours pull him back down. A few voices murmur their agreement; others drown them out. Judge Hutschneider uses his gavel.

'Quiet!' he shouts. 'Order! Order!'

Two guards are on the scene, seizing the protester by the arms and marching him out of the room. In her mind, Mia marks them on technical merit and execution: ten out of ten.

At the front of the room the next black mannequin is on his feet. Mia recognises her lawyer. In her opinion, Rosentreter is overplaying himself. His movements are tediously slow and clumsy and he pulls on his forelock with unnecessary force, apparently intent on removing his scalp. Less would be more.

'Your Honour,' says Rosentreter, 'bearing in mind the weight of evidence, the private counsel will not be speaking in Frau Holl's defence.'

The crowd gasps. For once, Rosentreter has come to court without his usual stack of files. He picks up a single sheet of paper, smooths it with his fingers and takes a deep breath. He looks like a schoolboy about to read a poem to the class.

'No one is obliged to become an enemy of the Method by representing persons identified by the Method as enemy combatants. Such persons are encouraged to represent themselves. Long live the Method. Santé.'

Rosentreter sits back down.

After such a lousy statement, Mia feels obliged to boo. She is joined by someone from the public gallery.

'It's a set-up!' calls a voice from the corner and falls silent. The guards have positioned themselves around the courtroom and are scanning the crowd.

'The court accepts the private counsel's right to self-defence,' says Judge Hutschneider loudly. 'Now, moving on to the evidence. Heinrich Kramer, please take the witness stand.'

Instead of a black mannequin, the next person to rise is a tall, slim figure with a proud profile and eyes as dark as night; a figure who has played the part of the only real person in Mia's life for days, or maybe weeks, or maybe all her life. As she follows Kramer's journey to the front of the courtroom, her eyes begin to water, not because of the atomisers, which are squirting disinfectant at her face. She has missed him.

'I swear by the Method to speak the truth, the whole truth, and so forth,' says Kramer as soon as he reaches the stand. 'After decades of hard work, we have arrived at a Method that guarantees to every citizen a long and happy life. Regrettably, not everyone appreciates our efforts. The enemies of happiness are numerous and deadly, but the Method will fight them! Our values will be protected.'

The spectators clap mechanically. Kramer nods and puts a finger to his lips to quell the noise.

Barker raises his voice to reinsert himself at the heart of the action. 'Herr Kramer, for the benefit of the court, could you describe your—'

'No one can claim to know the defendant better than I do,' Kramer interrupts him.

'It's true,' says Mia fondly.

'Frau Holl is an enlightened individual – intelligent and self-aware. A strong character.'

'Thank you, Heinrich,' says Mia.

'A former adherent of the Method, now a dangerous fanatic, Frau Holl is a crusader who wants to die for her cause. The maximum penalty is what she desires. The court respects her as a free human being. The punishment honours the criminal!'

Once again the spectators applaud, but no one applauds more vigorously than Mia.

'Hurrah!' shouts someone.

'Quiet, please,' says Hutschneider.

Mia nods, claps, cries and shakes her head. She claps so vigorously that she can no longer hear what is being said. At last she stops when three figures come into view. They are dressed in white tabards and walk nervously towards the judge, veering to the left and the right, ready to bolt at any moment. A guard leads them to the witness stand.

'Please raise your hands,' says Hutschneider. 'Do you swear to tell the truth, the whole truth and nothing but the truth?'

'We do,' says Lizzie.

'So help us God,' says Driss.

'Don't mention God,' hisses Pollie.

'My good ladies,' says Hutschneider, 'I call on you to testify that you were present when the defendant's apartment was searched.'

'We were, Your Honour,' says Lizzie.

'Mia is a martyr!' shouts Driss.

'Are you crazy?' whispers Pollie.

The spectators whisper and mutter. By now an army of guards has surrounded the public gallery. Several detach themselves and approach the stand.

'What Driss means,' says Lizzie quickly, 'is Frau Holl is a terrorist.'

'It's the same thing,' says Driss. 'A martyr and a terrorist!'

'Dirty sympathiser!' shouts a man from the public gallery, rising to his feet.

'Gag her!' shouts another, jumping up.

Hutschneider turns to the guards. 'Do your damn job!' he barks. 'Get the troublemakers out of my courtroom!'

Driss stares at the uniformed men with her vacant gaze.

'It was in the papers,' she tells them. 'But I knew all along: Mia is a good terrorist!'

'Traitor!'

'Get her out!'

'Adjourn the proceedings,' says one of the associate judges to Hutschneider. 'Clear the court!'

'The trial will continue!' calls Heinrich Kramer from among the reporters. 'We're finishing this today!'

'Quiet!' shouts Hutschneider.

'The Method is Murder!' someone shouts back.

The man who has just spoken is small with a bullet head and thinning hair. Mia thinks he is probably a programmer. The man sitting next to him drives a fist into his jaw. We can infer from the bullet head's expression that we are witnessing his first encounter with physical pain. Others join in while three guards charge towards them, grab the bullet head by the arms and drag him from the room.

'You are sacrificing Mia on the altar of your delusions,' cries someone else as the small man is lifted out.

'Hear, hear!' shouts Driss.

Several men are clambering over the railings towards the witness stand. The guards close in around Driss; the first handcuffs her, while his companions swing their batons to beat back the men. Mia watches as Driss is dragged to the door. The time has come for Mia's moment in the limelight. By rights, the speech should be given by Moritz, but since Moritz is absent, it falls to her. She rattles the bars furiously and the whole cage starts to shake.

'Quiet! Everyone, quiet! It's my turn!' Gradually, the activity in the courtroom dies down; heads turn towards her, and at last it is still.

'Raze the system to the ground,' says Mia. 'Tear down the edifice! Fetch the guillotine from the cellar and kill! Kill hundreds and thousands, plunder, rape, starve and freeze! The rest of you, hold your peace. You can call it what you like: cowardice or good sense. You can think of yourselves as private citizens, collaborators or disciples of the system, as apolitical or individual, as traitors to humanity or champions of humankind. It makes no difference. Kill or be quiet. The rest is theatre.'

'She's got some strange ideas for a fanatic,' says one of the associate judges in the ensuing silence.

'I thought I'd get more of a reaction,' says Mia. 'Aren't you going to applaud?'

'That does it,' says Hutschneider. Exhausted, he dabs his face with a handkerchief and wipes the sweat from his neck. 'I've heard enough. The defendant is making a mockery of this trial. The hearing is over. All that remains is for the defendant to answer a final question. Frau Holl, is there anyone you would like to be present when the sentence is imposed?'

'Heinrich Kramer,' says Mia promptly.

'I accept,' says Kramer.

'Splendid,' says Hutschneider. 'In that case, the verdict can be read.'

He opens a file to produce a document that we can assume was written before the hearing began.

Mia sits back in her cage, closes her eyes and smiles. 'Nevertheless,' she says softly, 'I still won.'

'First, the defendant is found guilty of anti-Method activities on the following counts: orchestrating a terrorist campaign, conspiring to cause civil unrest, unauthorised use of toxic substances, and non-participation in compulsory testing to the detriment of the general good. Second, the defendant is sentenced to freezing for an unlimited term. Third, the defendant is ordered to pay court fees and all associated costs. The court's decision was based on the following facts . . .'

See above. See above, see above and see above. See the beginning of the century, the end of the century, the middle of the century. See above.

Finished

It is possibly the most peaceful moment in weeks, or maybe months. The bed is comfortable, the room is clean, the temperature is regulated. Mia has been washed, massaged and fed. She has been dressed in a neoprene suit that protects the skin from frostbite. She has been carried in and placed on a machine that looks as harmless as a sunbed with its glass panels and tubes. Even Hutschneider and Kramer no longer look threatening; they look no larger or smaller than life. Kramer is cooling Mia's brow with a damp cloth. He checks she is lying comfortably and offers her a sip of hot water from a mug. It would be easy to imagine him tucking her up in a freshly laundered white duvet. Mia is tired. *Vita minima* or suspended animation. She thinks fearlessly of the slowing of her heartbeat, her increasingly irregular breath, the failure of her eyes. Mia knows it is merely the evaporation of lachrymal fluid during flash-freezing that takes away the human look, the absence of which inspires such dread. Who needs a look when there is nothing left to see? Even the spasms have almost stopped. What is the point of shaking your head if you don't know whom or what you are saying *no* to?

'Let it be noted,' says Hutschneider, 'that Frau Holl was informed of the medical implications in accordance with the Health Code, Article 234. The procedure was overseen by Judge Hutschneider. Also in attendance was Heinrich Kramer at the convict's request. The convict was given the opportunity to make a last request. Frau Holl, what is your final request?'

Mia is pleasantly weary; it takes a while for her to realise that he expects an answer. 'Do you really still ask that?'

'It's classical,' says Kramer.

'In that case, a classic request. I'd like a cigarette, please.'

Kramer is visibly delighted; he almost claps his hands with glee. 'Did you hear that?' he shouts. 'I knew it!'

He produces a silver cigarette case and offers it gallantly to Mia.

'You can't just—' protests the judge.

'You're a killjoy,' says Kramer, relaxed. He lights the cigarette.

Mia takes a long drag.

'The convict requested . . .' Hutschneider looks up from his notepad. 'I can't do it! Not in the official transcript.' He thinks for a moment. 'The convict declined the opportunity for a final request.'

Hutschneider writes it down. Then he signals to an invisible someone who is operating a contraption behind a pane of mirrored glass.

'I liked the speech about the guillotine,' says Kramer. 'Kill or be quiet. I'd like to quote it in the obituary, if I may. How do you feel?'

'I feel fine,' says Mia. 'It smells of Moritz.'

'In the name of the Method,' says Hutschneider.

Slowly, the lid of the apparatus descends. Mia takes another drag on the cigarette and hands it back to Kramer.

'So I'm being exiled,' she says softly.

The lid closes. We can't see much of Mia, just her feet. Cold mist escapes with a hiss through the gaps. Stepping back, Kramer and Hutschneider supervise from an appropriate distance.

This would be a good time for it to be finished, a good parting line. This is the most peaceful moment in weeks or even months.

But the door flies open. Barker rushes in, gasping for breath. In his hands is a document rolled up to form a scroll and sealed in the old-fashioned way.

'Your Honour!' he says, still panting. 'The judgment has been reversed.'

'Stop!' shouts Hutschneider.

At once the hissing stops and the cold mist begins to disperse.

'Thank the Method,' says Barker. 'That was close.'

'What's going on?' Hutschneider is so agitated that he almost snatches the scroll from the prosecutor's hand.

Barker breaks the seal.

Kramer is leaning against the wall in his customary style, arms crossed, with a satisfied smile.

'The President of the Method Council,' says Barker, reading aloud, 'has considered the defence's appeal and, at the urging of his most senior advisers, has agreed to a reprieve.'

The lid clicks open.

'Great news,' says Kramer. 'You're saved.'

Mia struggles to sit up. 'What?' she asks in a flat voice.

Kramer roars with laughter to see her dismay. He laughs so hard he can hardly breathe.

'Herr Kramer,' says an agitated Hutschneider, 'I don't understand . . .'

Kramer is too busy laughing to do anything but point at Mia. 'The condemned woman!' he splutters when he is finally able to talk. 'See how disappointed she is? She honestly thought the Method would turn her into a martyr. What kind of incompetent system creates cult figures to be worshipped by the fickle population? Jesus of Nazareth, Joan of Arc — death gave them immortality and lent weight to their cause. It's not going to happen to you, Frau Holl. Get up, put on your clothes, go home! You're . . .' He dissolves into laughter again. 'You're free!'

'No,' whispers Mia.

Barker, slowly catching on, twists his face into a grin.

'That's enough now.' Hutschneider glares furiously at Kramer, who wipes away the tears of laughter and regains his composure.

'No!' screams Mia. 'You can't do that! You've got to keep me here! You owe me that much!'

'Find her a psychologist,' says Barker to Hutschneider. 'Appoint a personal counsellor. Re-socialisation, that's the key. Put her in a home with medical supervision. She needs training for normal life.'

'Leave it to me,' says Hutschneider.

'Trust-building exercises. Political education. Method coaching.'

Still talking, the two men leave the room. Kramer's hand rests on the doorknob.

'Farewell, Frau Holl,' he says.

Mia, alone in the room, shakes her head.

For only now is she, only now is the game, only now is it all truly finished.

Juli Zeh was born in 1974 and lives in Brandenburg. She studied International Law, worked with the UN in New York, and completed her studies in Creative Writing. Juli Zeh has won numerous awards, including the international Per Olov Enquist Award and the French Prix Cévennes for Best European Novel. Her work has been translated into thirty languages.

Sally-Ann Spencer studied Modern and Medieval Languages at the University of Cambridge. She is the translator of several contemporary German novels, including Frank Schätzing's *The Swarm*, for which she was awarded the Schlegel-Tieck prize. At present she is working on a PhD on literary translation at the University of Victoria in Wellington, New Zealand.